Anna Livia

BULLDOZER RISING

Published by Onlywomen Press, radical feminist and lesbian publishers, 38 Mount Pleasant, London WC1X 0AP, England

The First, Second, Third and Fourth Sightings were first published in 'Conditions' 13. The Fifth, Sixth, Seventh and Ninth Sightings will be published in 'Common Lives/Lesbian Lives' 26, in April 1988. The Seventeenth Sighting will be published in 'Sinister Wisdom' 34.

Typeset by Columns of Reading, Berkshire
Printed and bound in Great Britain by Redwood Burn Ltd.,
Trowbridge, Wiltshire
Cover printed by Duxford Press, London

Cover illustration © Helen Manning

British Library Cataloguing in Publication Data

Livia, Anna, *1955–*
   Bulldozer Rising.
   I. Title
   823'.914 [F]

   ISBN 0–906500–27–3

for Lilian

I would like to take this opportunity to thank a number of lesbians and heterosexual women from whose work I drew much of the inspiration for this novel: Dodici Azpadu for writing *Goat Song*; Anna Wilson for *Altogether Elsewhere*; Lee Lynch for *The Swashbuckler*; Julia Penelope for *The Mystery of Lesbians*; Anna Kavan for *Asylum Piece*; Bertha Harris for *Lover*; and Frances Eileen Maud Pavier Brawn, my paternal grandmother commonly known as Bobs, for wearing the silver labyris and being an old battle axe until the bitter end.

All characters and events in this book are exactly as I remember them. Others may remember differently, this is my version.

First Sighting: SHIMMER HOSEN

Three youngwomen in a public toilet. Standard issue: lined with silver mirrors, trays of lurid lipgloss, eyestars, blusher, bloomer and blurrer in case of misplacement of cosmetic brainwave. The slats across each stall began a foot and a half from the floor and were only three feet high to prevent any illicit elixir drinking, resting or life-preserving. To prevent? To discourage, at least, all but the permitted defecation, micturition and such sexual combinations as were the fashion of the day, by the simple expedient of making all public. How, indeed, could the Citizens' Ordinances be enforced without total publicity?

The three youngwomen, since to be alive was to be young, were precisely eighty, eighty four and one quarter, ninety and one half seasons old which, as there are six seasons to every year, meant three females of thirteen, fourteen and fifteen respectively.

The three youngwomen took their places in the queue for the two available stalls. As they spurned the cosmetics, apart from a playful snort of nose powder, which caused not kicks but sneezes, it must be assumed they were there for evacuation.

"Queues should be outlawed," grumbled the youngest of the youngwomen.

"They have been. Citizens' Ordinance 4378," said the middle-aged youngwoman.

"Time wastage," added the oldest.

"Do you hear that?" whined the youngest at the two closed doors of the stalls. "You're wasting our time."

No answer was forthcoming, so she contented herself with lifting one satiny thigh and plunging her creamy toes in the blue lipgloss. She proceeded to scrawl the profanity "CANCER" in large, sloppy letters across the silver mirrors. Her two friends smiled admiration, though the oldest seemed insufficiently aware of her advanced years, for her gaze was vague and introspective. She had recently, it is true, been in a kinky relationship with a woman twice as old as she, and so had for some time been on the receiving end of any admiration going. Still, were these laurels to rest upon? The youngest increased her aerobic jiggling.

At last one of the stalls opened and the first, she of middle years, dived in. The second door did not open. Despite the furious glances of the remaining youngwomen, it remained steadfastly shut. Close scrutiny threw up nothing unusual in the arrow-pointed stilettoes, pink and puce shimmer hosen and elongated ankles of the present incumbent. Such ankles could not be natural, she had certainly undergone body-sculpture, but then, what youngwoman had not these days? What youngman, for that matter?

The two youngwomen mused for a while on the alluring possibility of a man on their turf, but the thought soon paled, and when even jiggling and showing her knickers lost its appeal, the youngest, who should, by rights, have gone first, shrieked loudly,

"I think someone died in there."

Now this did produce an effect. The arrow-pointed stilettoes drew themselves up sharply and the shimmer hosen was yanked over sculptured calves with no little risk of snagging. A sure sign of acute anxiety, the price of shimmer hosen these days. But still the occupant did not emerge.

Encouraged by her previous success, the youngest youngwoman accused, half triumph, half indignation, "She's resting."

At this final indignity, the toilet flushed, the trimmed ankles stood upon spikey heels, and the bolt was drawn. Shortly after, the other toilet flushed and the middle-aged youngwoman emerged about the same time as her neighbour. The youngest of the young could have bolted for that compartment and relieved herself, but rage and curiosity had hold of her. She allowed the oldest of the youngwomen to pass in front, her own eyes fixed on the wearer of the pink and puce shimmer hosen.

The stranger was weeping. Large, beautiful tears collected and splashed down her face. By the looks of the work that had been done on her, she must have been very rich indeed. Every operation, by-pass, graft, uplift, transplant known to the modern knife had been performed. The result was truly gorgeous.

The youngest of the young was taken aback at the sight of such sobbing splendour. Emotion energises, and this creature had put her through the gamut from admiration and mirth to wrath and bladder retention. All might still have passed off as the normal events of a heightened day if the weeper had only encouraged the youth's sexual suggestions, but she seemed incapable. Or revulsed.

The youth recognised something: hesitation? fatigue? Not revulsion, certainly, but as certainly not the fulsome come-on she was used to.

"You!" she spluttered, "You nearly made me wet myself. I would have had to walk around like an old-woman or an incontinent. You were resting, I know you were."

An involuntary flicker passed across the weeper's face.

"You've done well with the cosmetic surgery," pursued the youth, "but I wonder, now, was any of it life-preserving?"

The last two words were spat with malicious

triumph as the youth grabbed the weeper's head, spun the hot tap full on, and commenced dousing her victim. The weeper said nothing. Pain? Exhaustion? Terror? Or sexual thrill at indignity? The youth did not pause to discover. The water in the pipes ran scalding hot, peeling a brown layer off the weeper's face. A skin foundation? The youth yanked the head back by the hair. An enormous birds' nest came away in her hands, along with some grey straggles. The youth screamed surprise, and then horror as she saw that without the wig, her playmate was an old, old woman. Should have been long dead. Well over forty one. Years, not seasons.

In the interval of the scream, three things happened. The oldest youngwoman reappeared from the toilet. The middle-aged youngwoman got tired of waiting. The youngest youngwoman began, indeed, to wet herself. She could not afford to go around wet with urine, so she spat,

"Keep her for me. Let her wait for punishment. Think how many've gone before just so's she could reach that age."

The oldest of the young looked at the very old woman: disgust, pity and interest equally mingled.

"Come on," she whispered urgently, "I'll get you a car. You can use my PIN number and I've plenty cosmetics so you can get homesafe." The oldwoman allowed herself to be supported out of the toilet and guided to a car. She accepted a blue scarf as a veil till she could rebuild her face.

The two women walked down the steps arm in arm like lovers. The oldwoman found herself lifted off the high kerb with a dance-step twirl. Her partner spared only a few thoughts for the trouble she'd be in if they were reported or the PIN number traced. By good luck, a car idled at the kerb; the driver merely mumbled from his screen, not looking up.

"Now you get in," instructed the oldwoman.

"Oh, of course. I'll see you homesafe. Besides, you'll need me to see to your face."

"No," said the oldwoman shortly, "I've done it myself these last fifty years."

Years, she said, not seasons.

"You take this car," she insisted, "I'll make my own way."

"Don't you trust me?" sulked her escort.

"No," the oldwoman repeated, waving the car off.

Second Sighting: SUPERMAZE

Citizens' Ordinance 4378 banned queues on grounds of time wastage. Since they had only one and forty years apiece, no-one should spend a moment waiting, the citizens argued. All Now became second only to All Public. Since shortages, of whatever commodity had caused the queue in the first place, remained undiminished, and since this was a city of appearance and adaptation, the citizens learned to regard waiting time as unscheduled leisure for which contingency they prepared carefully before leaving homesafe. Those who revelled in the interpersonal possibilities of public transport leapt joyfully from skateboard to bus platform at a passing traffic light. Nobody waited at a bus stop unless they had a fresh ground coffee, a hot croissant and the morning's paper.

[And many's the passing forty who fed solely on the cream and crumbs departing buses left in their wake. Some followed the bus routes as the poor of old had followed a horse, shovelling shit with thankful hearts.]

Those who made assignation at the raw meat counter at Floggins Supermaze might idle at the check-out, eyeing up the talent. They must not stare anxiously at their watches, count their change or complain. Watches were to measure speed-up, not stand-still. Only the old complained and, since to be alive was to be young, the good citizens knew to grin and turn every eventuality into a sensual experience.

Seventeen youngpeople stood in a row behind a cash-desk obediently eyeing up the talent. They carried metal baskets full of cream-spray, sugar-fix, butterburgers and other staples. Most were reading the paper. The names varied, but all papers gave the same news, honing the wording to suit the sexual range of the populace. Thus a new Citizens' Ordinance that all kerbs be raised to a height of two feet to reduce the wheelchair menace read:

KERB-CRAWLERS CURBED

Affirmative action has been taken by a far-sighted citizenry to stop the present use of wheels to replace rickety legs. 'Basket cases have been known to preserve mobility', said a spokecit, 'enhancing their morale and possibly continuing their own lives beyond natural departure, at we know not what cost to scarce resources. When pigeons threatened to coat the city with lime, we coated the window-sills with acid: without feet the birds could not run amok. We answer logic with logic.'

Twenty Twenty Vision, mouthpiece of the
moment

In *Necrophilos*, progressive journal for sex with the dying, the same item was headlined: TAKE YOUR FILL AT THE CROSSROADS. Coverage may be imagined.

One youngman ostentatiously opened a copy of *Objectivity*, the Ackademick paper, and made a valiant attempt to look as though he were slumming in the Supermaze.

While one might understand the desire of those who have outlived their natural span to prolong their existence, nevertheless we are not obliged to pander to it. The faculty for abstract understanding should not mislead us into injustice. Civic priorities have declared the optimum death date to be forty one years of age; let us not favour those anti-social elements who live beyond it at the expense of the under forties. High kerbs may justly be regarded as a municipal metaphor for high morals.

At the next cash-desk, there were only two young people and a sign: THREE ITEMS OR LESS. The sign was spotted simultaneously by three youngwomen from the first cash desk: a couple and a single. The single roller-skated, the couple waltzed. The single reached the second cash desk after the quick quick, youngwoman but before her slow slow, partner. She was therefore surrounded by their conversation.

"Did you see that?"

"Inhuman."

"Horrendous. Might rub off on you. All that loose skin."

"Wouldn't wanna get near it, let alone lick it."

"What I don't understand is why they go on after they get like that. They know no one wants them."

"I'm shooting up and sailing the car over Pit's Parapet in my burn out year. Got a peer wants to come with."

"That's nice." (Pause). "I saw one once, you know."

"Sure it wasn't sunburn?"

"No, honestcitizen. It was down the market. She was buying fruit. They'd run out of injected apples but she said, no matter, she'd take them untreated, add the supplements at home."

"They're not allowed to sell uninjected fruit. Citizens' Ordinance 4378b."

"Precisely. That's what put me onto her. These old ones can't eat anything else. They say their stomachs..."

"Don't swear."

"Well, they can't digest: cream, sugar, fairy floss, chocolate chivers, anything. And they can't sleep; not past six o'clock in the morning."

"Didn't know there was a six o'clock in the morning."

"Elbows, knuckles, knees, neck, back . . . all the places you bend, they're stiff. And they swell. And they shrink. And they go a funny colour: brown spots if they're white; grey if they were black. And all their hair goes white. And their teeth fall out, and their eyes get covered over, and when they fall, their bones just crumble."

"Why you telling me all this? Make me lose my appetite."

"I just don't understand it. Why they don't bliss out quietly on an overdose. No one's asking them to spill kerosene all over themselves if they don't choose."

"Be fair. Most citizens have a ball, burn out and bliss out. How many selfish old baskets do you see hobbling along the travelators?"

"I get this feeling there are more of them than there was."

"One is more than there should be and there's the community service to deal with them."

The shimmer hosen stretched tight in the public toilet. Fifty five years of air that oldwoman had breathed. Was it pity that helped her escape, the single youngwoman wondered, or faulty citizenship? Should she track her down and turn her in?

Third Sighting: SPARKLERS

Out of the mouth of an underpass glided a youngwoman on one leg, the other was raised behind her,
silver skate glinting at ear height, in shimmering
arabesque. Not only beauty and fragility, but the
necessary angle of trajectory to avoid wind friction
and premature spin. The underpass vomited onto a
six lane highway guarded by a roundabout. The
resulting crosscurrents could blow over a hoverpad,
let alone a human figure naked but for flesh and lurex
one ply. This figure had long, heavy legs, a powerful
back and light, gracious arms as though they did no
more than welcome you to the show. On solid ground
she would have been a plain, rather unremarkable
Tramontane, but here, amongst the streak and flow of
the traffic, she moved like liquid mercury.

Her thighs stored the momentum of the ascent: the
underpass was too narrow to attempt anything creative
and the skaters only used it as a starting boost. The air
was cold and empty after the hugging clamour of the
concrete; with the exhilaration of new paint and a
clean canvas, Zay noted the absence of other skaters.
She began at once to weave eights and spirals into the
rigid rectilinear display before her. She struck a skate
against a stationary wheel hub: by dint of steel on

steel, the sparklers on her bodysuit caught light. To the straight lines of white headlamps and red tail-lights was added this sudden silver spray. Horns honked, brakes screeched, drivers swore and fellow skaters applauded. Shoppers, strollers and eaters paused: life was short, art even shorter. For a moment all the smooth lines of traffic wobbled into abrupt angles with the shower of sparklers dancing around them. It was such, short, perfect moments which showed, more than a volume of words, a week of speeches, the true value of the youth culture. This was the apex of artistic achievement, a symbol for life itself.

Bus passengers crowded to the back for a closer look. A pity, but it takes impeccable timing to orchestrate a city street and Zay, now speeding backwards, sensed that her busking time was up; she should sign her work and bow off. A warning shout would introduce a completely new theme, unseemly in the closing bars of the last movement. As Zay drew alongside the bus, the more musical passengers realised her intent, and improvised a retreat, but not all, and not soon enough. Zay leapt forward, the heavy skates weighing her down, cumbersome as storks' legs, until, like a stork, she found her balance in the air and caught the platform pole with startling grace. Around she spun, into the bus and out again. Her usual signature.

A sudden blow to the back of the neck caused one youngman to tumble from the platform into the road. As a red rapidojet screeched forward, power shorting, the youngman's fellow passengers shot a swift glance, seeking some sign of illness or disability which would make this untimely death more palatable. As the wheels claimed him, a purple welt was noted upon his neck. So, the man was a sickie, unworthy of their nascent sympathy. As the hard tyres broke the soft body, the passengers tutted over internalised anger, emotional constipation.

Zay, surrounded by fellow citizens showing their

appreciation, PIN-numbers at the ready, was unable to see the road, though it was soon apparent from his white gown that an Ack Ack had been called. Zay caught only stray sentences of what was clearly the life oration.

"Citizens do not fear . . . presence of death amongst us. . . . No . . . insists on the significance of life . . . scarce resources . . . to more deserving . . . healthy, youthful . . . only a drain on. . . . Ugly, misshapen . . . timely end."

Zay had heard it all before. They had all heard it before but the Ack Acks' speech never failed in its task of reassurance. Zay hoped the Ack would stick around, she had something to ask.

"This beautiful youngwoman . . . fabulous display . . . superb athlete." So he'd gone onto her. Good. That'd increase the credits. And indeed the citizens pressed round her tighter than before till she almost concluded the best art ends in a death. With the arrival of a band of Tramontanes, hoses in hand, Zay managed to slip away. Better not risk that comparison.

"Scuse me, cit, word in your ear?"

"In my ear, youngwoman? Now you can do better than that."

"Wherever," said Zay, "with skates on."

The Ack Ack paused to consider.

"What's the trade?"

"Ackademic credit."

"Teach a Tramontane to read, you never hear the last of it."

But he led the way.

Zay thought how much easier it might be as a cleaner in the Ackademy. Skaters were artists and artists could only get credit. Hard cash debases. Reputation sharpens performance.

When the Ack was through, Zay asked for her numbers.

"Come, come. You know this sort of thing is entirely counter-indicated. Ackademicks and Tramontanes: it'd never do."

"We just did it."

"Don't be coarse."

"I am coarse. I'm a Tramontane."

"Ackademic credit! Next you'll be asking for a distinction." Zay raised her left leg to pirouette. She rotated an elegant ankle.

"You know you have a grey patch over your right temple?" she challenged, and with a sharp jerk she cut off a lock on the rim of her skate.

"I'll have you before a tribunal," threatened the Ack, "Tramontanes are very low priority."

"Shouldn't you be preparing for your burn-out?" Zay dangled the thin white hair in front of him.

"I'm only 240 seasons."

"I'd be forgiven for not realising that," Zay retorted, silver skate shooting out odd gleams of reflected light. "Now, that distinction you mentioned?"

The group of Tramontanes aimed their hoses at the high kerb, squirting the remains of the youngman into the gutter. There was much that would not flow through the narrow grating and had to be scooped up by hand. Warm, soft lumps. Vomit swirled and eddied with the pink of watery blood. Ack Acks were accorded two leisure days for the responsibility of dealing with death. Tramontanes got to leave work early.

Fourth Sighting: MARBLED ENDPAPERS

Fine weather, moonlight and a three road roundabout were the essentials for a book trade. At the conjunction of these three requisites books and traders materialised. Though medium priority, books were regarded with great suspicion in some quarters. More than one influential spokecit had suggested downgrading. There was no objection to the numerous "Citizens' Wellbeing" manifests; these were available at the checkout of every supermaze. The current flood of SEXUAL SURGERY and COOKING FOR FATHERHOOD tracts were at least leaflet formula: short, snappy and no nasty verbs. It was, not to put too fine a point on it, the old books which caused problems; no amount of euphemising about the 'twice-young', the 'ever-green' or the 'well-thumbed' could change things. They were long, they had no pictures; what's more, they were manufactured in some distant age before the present citizens were born. The maxim of All Public prevailed: book trades could take place, but only in the open air, in a public concourse.

Zay jumped from kerb to roadway and began spiralling in as she skated round the roundabout. By the third spin she had reached the centre island. Her blue scarf she had given to the oldwoman in the toilet, but concealment would have been difficult anyway under the combined onslaught of motorway lighting and roving spots. These were so bright, so glaring that they created huge monsters by the starkness of their shadows. Perhaps Zay's singularity would be dismissed as overkill, not the sharp features of the Tramontana. Perhaps citizens whose vision was tunnelled to the books of the long-dead had not scope for such observations.

All around yelled at Zay to think, eat, move, breathe, live faster. Where time was essence, speed was wealth. Credit bought that precious commodity: altruistic time, measured units of the lives of fellow citizens, as invested in numerical promises to the bearer. Whilst it would not be true to say that the citizens were cannibals, in the proper sense, yet an Ack Ack could consume the life of a Tramontane. Though destined to live but forty years apiece, the unit hour of the former had a higher exchange rate than the unit hour of the latter. Zay, determined not to be eaten alive, had put her skates on and assimilated.

The citizens' trade with the Tramontanes was just and rigorously logical, according to the highest principles. If zurbans wished to live in the city as Tramontanes, then their unit hour must have the lowest possible value. In a city where time is rationed to maximise enjoyment, outsiders must be rationed doubly, to compensate for the unrationed time they spend elsewhere. In fact, the Tramontane hour set a minimum. If, on the other hand, they wished to shed zurban ways, they were at liberty to assimilate, enjoying a market hour like any other citizen. Precisely what constituted zurbanity had never been successfully codified, but common sense prevailed: the most apparent feature of zurbans was the fact that they came from outside the city. Should they persist in this coming, which of course entailed also a going, then they could quite rightly be considered outsiders. Once this coming and going stopped, full citizenship could begin. In case this led to confusion and muddled thinking, it was clarified that as citizens had not come from elsewhere in the first place, they were free to come and go as they liked.

Zay, Tramontane solely through her mother-vessel, felt no burning desire to go exurbs, which was said in any case to be all scrub and sterility: a place where nothing moved, nothing sounded, where the pavement was flat and gravity heavy. No fear. Common sense declared a secondary characteristic of zurbanity to be the tendency to clan together; the post-assimilatory Zay steered well-clear of other Tramontanes. She had spent many of her zurban minimum hours on book, screen and stereo credits eager to absorb what she could of this youthful city, which was so exciting and so liberating, so open and egalitarian, and which still seemed new to her, being born not of but under it. The cassettes and reels were as slick and fast produced as the carbodies on the street; only the books had taken time. Someone else's time. The older, the longer. Zay thrilled to finger a hand-tooled leather cover, a hand-sewn binding, the thick, yellowy wadding and fraying edges of home pulped paper.

Strange, in a city of spectators, performers and applauders, a city which devoted its concentrated attention to its fellow citizen, that such solipsistic, abstemious enjoyment should be tolerated. But toleration was the keyword of this open city. Throughout the book trade a hundred silent admirations were in progress, a hundred covetings. The headlamps of cars on the roundabout threw a passing yellow pool over this or that book trader, setting each more apart than before.

As it entered the roundabout and came toward the island, one such yellow beam flooded Zay's back, casting her shadow gigantic over the traders. As it swerved round to the left, the beam widened over a trestle and Zay's attention was drawn to a thick brown volume at the back of the stand. She picked it up. It was an old zurban atlas. Very old; the work of a quarter lifetime: letterpress with hand-inked maps, marbled endpapers and a gold-embossed thumb key cut into the side of the pages. Had she a sense of smell, Zay would have detected real kid and a hundred years of dust.

"Pursuing your extra-mural studies?" joked a trader.

Zay smiled obediently. Then she flicked the fly-leaf.

"Please return to Ithaca Benaccar."

"Where did you get this?" she demanded.

"Fair trade," said the trader. "What's it to you? You can't afford it."

"What you asking?"

"What you got?"

No point stalling; you didn't bargain over this one.

"Ackademic distinction."

The trader whistled. "What you do to get that? Suck an Ack Ack? You must be good."

Zay thought of the lumps of flesh in the gutter. And of the oldwoman in her blue veil. Strange how death happens and doesn't happen.

"I'll take it," Zay said.

"Will you now?"

"Yes, now," Zay repeated firmly, seizing the book and quoting her credits. She reeled them off just fast enough for the trader to have to concentrate. Then she skated away.

Ithaca Ithaca Ithaca said her skate wheels as they clicked. They should not have been clicking at all. Ithaca Benaccar. Ithaca Benaccar. Please return to.

"Ithaca," Zay bleated. An unlikely noise for such a big woman, and she realised she was frightened. What had forced Ithaca to part with the atlas? What had they done to her? What had who done? A thousand faceless citizens jumped for buses, sprang up kerbs, ate sugarfix and urinated in toilets. Ithaca would never trade that atlas unless her life depended on it. Was it a clearance sale? Were all the books on that stall Ithaca's? Zay set her face full ahead, steered a plumb line between the two white parallels painted along the middle of the road. Her course was fixed: she would obey the inscription in the atlas and return to Ithaca Benaccar.

Fifth Sighting: SEEKERS OF SILVER LININGS

The oldwoman watched till the car was swallowed up in traffic. Her rescuer was unlikely to U turn back across six lanes. Karlin ached with irony. Here was a road with no underpass within a hundred stretches, a road which flowed like a treacherous torrent between her and homesafe, a road it was only advisable to cross by car. Karlin regretted the necessity for mistrust, she regretted the necessity of making her own way and, above all, she regretted the necessity of waving the car off.

At the pedestrian crossway youngpeople ran, vaulted, dared, dived and stonefaced their passage over. Leaning against the high kerb stood five bags of rubbish waiting for a shoal of citlets or, preferably, an advanced pregnancy to walk by. Karlin clambered down painfully to join them. If she jumped she feared she might break her knees which could no longer stand the shock of reinforced concrete. She covered herself closely in Zay's blue veil and thus, to all appearance, a blue laundry bag crumpled, tipped and sprawled into the road amongst the assorted garbage customarily littering the gutters of the city, despite a welter of Tramontane shovelling.

While awaiting an opportunity of making a dent in

the traffic, youngpeople played leapfrog over the firmer bags. Karlin flopped to the ground and spilled a little, as uninviting a bollard as possible. It would be hard to stand up again but for now she could take the weight off her feet; by this time in her exhaustion she could no longer feel them: two lumps of dead meat in mounds of spiked wadding. As though her nervous system had recorded the agony of an amputation, storing the moment in the nerve endings of her spinal cord long after both legs had been severed. Hot water, a lover's gentle hands could smooth them out, assure them no such trauma had taken place. There was no hot water present, but Karlin soon felt the hands of a fellow baglady, kneading and caressing, locating the exact place. Karlin lifted the icy fingers of a neighbour to her armpits, warming and reviving. Along the kerb two more old bags leaned together, for all the world like two old ladies propping each other up.

Consider the chameleon. How it changes colour with its environment: dark green on the camellia leaf, orange on the dirt road, brown on the jacaranda branch, grey on the frangipani. Hidden from prey and predator alike. Behold the chameleon, those enormous, protuberant eyes, coning to a pinpoint, how they swivel 180 degrees giving it eyes in the back of its head. Watch the saurian grace of the chameleon, how four hands and a tail hold the branch, letting go only one at a time, maintaining always a tight grip. See how it moves forwards slowly, smoothly, edging back and forth, shifting the delicate balance of its weight. Now its long tongue uncoils from its mouth and darts out, snaring the unwary victim on the sticky tip.

The old bundles disengaged when they heard the citlets coming. Many oldwomen considered their physical infirmities an emblem of humanity, slowing the body down sufficiently to make it notice the million small things around it, and which the anaesthetic speed of the citizens obviates or destroys. This was no rejoicing, more a seeking of silver linings and a carrying on despite. Oh a great carrying on despite.

Perhaps the origin of the epithet 'spiteful' in reference to the old.

Do not underestimate the chameleon. It can wait for hours. It can go a long time without food and is said even to live on air. It chooses the background which will camouflage it best.

A mixed crocodile of nellies and zappers climbed self-consciously, if nimbly, down the protruding bricks of the kerb.

By now the rubbish was sorted into more or less separate bags, though one still sloped sideways into the neck of another, slumping in the middle as though a woman held her lover's waist, a tenderly supported arm across a willing shoulder. As soon as the cars noted the citlet crocodile's approach, they stopped sharp and the waves opened like an urban Red Sea. Respect for extreme youth? Or respect for the wealth of the father-possessor? A little of both, tripled with healthy sexual interest in such highly-prized game, intended as it was for other eyes, other tongues. Not the same awed reverence with which a pregnancy was sighted, for potential must be held dearer than the breathing outcome whose material formation has already ruled out so many other possibles. Nevertheless, the stilling of the traffic allowed the old bags to cross the street at the leaden pace necessary to escape detection as living beings and provoke no comment more emotional than a citizenly sigh at the litter blowing in the road, and the usual curses on the slovenliness of the Tramontanes.

The eyes of the citizens are mesmerised by constant and giddying speed. Their focus must make perpetual adjustment to keep up, causing it to flicker, even when at rest, with the anxious twitch of the passenger gazing out from a moving gazibus. City eyes are so finely tuned to subtleties of fast living that below a certain level slow motion looks like suspension.

Sixth Sighting: RELISH

An oldwoman wrapped in a blue veil insinuated herself into the whirlpool of the central concourse to the northbound travelator. Such was the stramash that she found herself flung back out further down even than her entrypoint. She had lived too long to panic; one cursory glance strengthened her resolve not to die amidst such vacant agitation. Instead she waited, back to the wall, till she spotted a small concavity where she would not be jostled. She slid along, shoulder to shiny tile, and watched.

A youngman passed within an inch. Her chance. She stepped forward into the wake of his broad shoulders and jutting elbows. No one messed with a youngman in his prime. At each corner, or parting of the corridors, where another whirl of travellers struggled to remain on course despite equally determined efforts by the elbows of oncomers, the youngman thrust challengingly into the fray and the oldwoman shifted to the protection of his offside, keeping faithful pace. The tick in the ear of the rhinoceros. A complicated polka.

Karlin had herself thus propelled onto the travelator, deposited on its rushing belt, wedged securely between the hefty, unconscious flank of her protector and a large cardboard box, upon which she now sank. Sheer force of will had got her legs this far. She had lived on will a long time. There was a leaden numbness about her face, her left eye dragged at the corner and she knew from the great weight of her tongue in her mouth that she could not speak without slurring. She minded these more than all other symptoms. Hers was such a sweet honey-rolling voice; her eyes were as brown as river clay and as sharp as paprika. A person of clotted speech and lazy eye was scarcely human, had nothing with which to force her humanity upon the world.

Each oldwoman knew from frightening, isolated experience that not everyone died at forty one, but until she met, passed, glimpsed others of her age, she could not know she was not the only miserable hanger-on. Karlin's blow-out year had come and gone and still she felt no desire to do the decent thing. In this the city's commonplaces did it disservice. Karlin had heard say so often that by forty those citizens who had not dropped from exhaustion or saturation noticed the slowing of age upon them and wanted only to be spared long debilitation, that she believed it, waited to feel the way she felt she ought to feel. She waited so long she reached fifty without the first deathpang.

Certainly her body changed and certainly the city changed toward it, but not as much, perhaps, as for a woman who found it less easy to pass. For Karlin was beautiful. The youngwomen in the public toilet were wrong. Karlin's ankles, nor her thighs, nor her neck had ever touched a knife. They had never needed to: she was naturally slender. This single fact of her physical perfection had done more to isolate Karlin in the terror of her living forties than any new and horrifying blemish. Karlin thought she was exceptional, dreaded becoming the rule. Meanwhile each mouthful of food consumed was sucked from the skull of the young; each breath of air was poison gas blown into the throat of the young; each stolen

30

travelation knee-capped young joints. The brown spots on her hands, the wrinkles round her neck, the white hairs on her head made her sick with loathing and with fear, until the day she realised.

Soren Kesh would say that Karlin Miray realised precisely nothing but ran around dressed like a silly little nelly, sucking the young, spurning the old, until the day she required what only oldwomen could give. Karlin would reply that Soren was jealous, had always been jealous, because Karlin looked young, precocious even, at any age while Soren was quite as fat as a Tramontane.

A skateboard soared overhead, Karlin glanced back at her fellow travellers. The belt was packed and the walk lane was blocked, hence the skateboard's impatient leap. In rush hours the crowd stretched from one end of the travelator to the other, might easily have been termed 'a queue' were it not for the archival material posted along its perimeters by a far-sighted citizenry, making of public transport a ride-in museum. Karlin had shuddered at the implications of the display the first score times of seeing it; it was as much part of her make-up as the value of youth and the power of a waistline.

Instead she began to notice a woman only a few people back. First she noticed the woman's size. She was huge. Reminiscent of Ithaca the Enormous, only this woman was fat. Very, very fat. She was so big and so fat that she seemed the only real creature in the place. Beside her huge and rippling arms, her impressively solid legs – now crossed so that the diamond of pelvis, knees and feet appeared the foundations of some massy edifice – all the other thin, miserly forms were insubstantial tracings. Karlin's hand touched her own jagged hips, her jutting cheeks and the chest which was all ribcage: hard, begrudging bone.

Next Karlin noticed the woman was eating. From a basket by her sturdy right ankle she had picked out what looked very much like a ball of marouli-fruit.

31

Karlin could see that the skin had been grilled just long enough to brown without losing the silvery scales. The woman ate with care, decision and evident enjoyment. As purposefully she munched a salad of grated kerris with milnuts and thrace, chewing a few pitted ovals for a saltier taste. She looked neither guilty nor defiant. She ate.

Karlin felt pangs of what she could only call hunger. She reached automatically for an amphetamine before remembering that in her present state they would kill her, and that Soren had argued her out of them. The fat woman now broached a generous piece of very chocolatey fudge cake. Such enthusiasm, such relish, such tremendous life going on round that neat picnic basket. Karlin wanted it: the life, the food, the woman who could be that fat in that city and still eat so fulsomely in public.

"You give me strength," Karlin whispered as her exit approached. For barely one moment did she worry that the fat woman might denounce her. Surely the fat were as wasteful as the old, and a fat woman who could turn her back on a lifetime of "Save fuel, light an oboe" must have seen through some of the city's sentiments.

"Give me strength," echoed in the fat woman's ears. Even half-blind cripples could dribble insults if you were fat in this open city. But let them watch out, let them all watch out.

Seventh Sighting: SUDDEN GLINTS OF LIGHT

Away from the deep city the street was tall, cool and glassy quiet. The sun shot sudden dazzling reflections as it glanced off an occasional glint of window. Chrome shutters threw light back and forth in mirrored diagonals up and down the road. The highway in front of one tall, silent building lit up in a brisk catherine wheel, the heavy revolving door had begun to move, at last. Someone was leaving the building. All definition of object and colour had blurred hopelessly, only the distinction of light and shade remained to Karlin. She waited in her small insignificance till the revolutions slowed sufficiently for her to slip into a wedge and enter her block. That the old, who have less time to lose, should spend so much of it waiting, there must be a stronger word than irony.

It was nearing two p.m. At her best at five in the morning, Karlin was close to crumbling. Why was dawn the given hour for the undead to disintegrate? Those suckers of the pure blood of youth, whose victims' worst fate is to follow them and age in their turn. Noon, surely, is the real winnow. Karlin crossed the vast wastes of the marble foyer with the air of one who believes herself alone and relaxes smiling muscles into pain. She no longer cared whether she was observed. Not political defiance but physical incapacity. Simple economics: that extra iota of energy she might have spent caring, she'd already paid out elsewhere. She groped her way round the cold, smooth walls to the pater noster. The hum of its ceaseless progress up and down the lift shaft muffled Karlin's gasps for air. As soon as one of the platforms levelled with the ground floor, she must step neatly onto it and be whisked upwards. Karlin felt for the next platform with her foot, forgetting the heavy numbness of her nerve ends, moved forward and realised only as she fell that she had mistimed.

The pater noster carried her up, humming relentlessly, to the seventh floor. Usually a reassuring sound, proclaiming the good health of the city's powerhouse. Pointless to try standing again when she would be at just as much of a loss getting out at her flat. Karlin concentrated on counting floors, blocking out other considerations. Smells would have called out to the permanently blind Soren: disinfectant on level one; polish, level two; fresh paint caught in the ventilators, level five. But Karlin's blindness was too new and her body had suffered too recently from the diet of the city to recover other senses quickly. When her floor arrived, Karlin tumbled onto the mosaic, dragged her arm up the doorframe, pressed the thumbhole, and crawled into homesafe.

The use of thumbprints, the last word in safety because one hundred per cent unique, had overnight replaced the newly archaic key or voxon. Not till morning was it discovered that the delicate pattern of an onion skin suited the purpose admirably, overloading the mechanism and gaining access. Back to hope, faith and the bye-laws of probability. A city based on hope is no bad thing.

In different parts of the building taps dripped, pipes rumbled, meters clicked. In the street litter fluttered, water raced along gutters. Karlin's heart beat determinedly, her breath warmed her upper lip, cooled her

34

nostrils. Everywhere electricity hummed. It is unclear how many hours ticked away between Karlin's collapse at her own bedside and the arrival of Soren and Essa. Cold and dark crept together across the floor toward the body. Karlin felt a pinch at her ribs, light but insistent, not to be ignored. "I know that," she thought when the pinch came again. The cold spread up from her feet along her right hand side, her eyes no longer strained to register light from dark. "That's death," she thought. "Not yet, maybe, but it's there." Though numb from cold, she was not uncomfortable. Only motion hurt and move she could not.

Two heavy bodies stumbled off the pater noster. They paused, must have applied an onion skin to the thumbhole for presently the flat door swung open and steps resounded along the passageway. Once a method had been established whereby two oldwomen might lift a third, albeit very light, oldwoman without straining backs or causing pain, Karlin found herself tenderly rolled under her own thick duvet. The feathers of which had been gleaned, cleaned and unclotted over three seasons and night-time trips to the abattoir. Still Karlin shivered. She was swaddled in aertex, overtex and underdown. A hot water bottle was applied to the blocks of ice which melted into feet.

"What else?" asked Soren Kesh.

"She must eat," said Essa Foujad.

"No," Karlin managed on automatic pilot. She would waste the effort of somehow opening her mouth wide enough to take a spoon, keeping food on her tongue long enough to break it up, forcing her throat to pass sustenance down into her stomach, because she would vomit, an activity vital to keep to a minimum. If she did not vomit she would, in a short while, need to urinate. How was that to be managed? She had no idea how to tell her tongue to ready itself behind her upper teeth prior to articulation, but 'no' she had been practising for the last fifty four years, and 'no' she said to Essa. Then she rested.

"Record symptoms," Karlin instructed. Extraordinary this desire in the dying to leave tracks.

Each day Karlin dictated and Soren taped. Each day it seemed Karlin could do nothing for herself until the next day what small functions she had still been able to perform were further eroded. By the end of the third week she could no longer turn over in bed nor lift her head from the pillow. Soren recorded symptoms without the benefit of dictation. When Karlin vomited, which she did frequently though unable to eat for some time, her head fell limply from side to side and must be held by kind attendants. Karlin was fortunate, she had attendants.

Beautiful black swans swallow the lead lures cast by the city's anglers; their central nervous systems are so damaged that they cannot send the necessary impulses out to their muscles; their long and graceful necks trail limply in the water, causing their death by drowning.

When Karlin's jaw became too weak to bite, her throat too weak to swallow, her friends spent the precious mornings picking over the streets, mindful to move with the slow deliberation which seems to escape the ever-flickering eye of the young. Before they rest, they steam and mash vegetables into wet puree. There are always several bottlesful in the plastic bags which hang from Karlin's window over the car park. Puree is best kept cool; the dry, constant heat of the central booster encourages microbes and, though fridges are fitted with every kitchen unit, Karlin has not credit to cover the extra electricity.

Despite fear of age contagion and a clash of utopic visions; because of fierce argument and long-requited, long-surfeited lust, Karlin and Soren remain life friends. Essa is Soren's lover: this is not the best moment for Karlin to take a dislike. Soren is not too fond of Karlin's latest lovely either, calls Karlin an age traitor for bringing a youngwoman amongst them. And where is Ithaca now, Soren nods to Essa, now that she is needed?

Eighth Sighting: HANGING GAZIBUS

A half-empty, off-peak, hanging gazibus plunged toward the city from the hinterland, stopping at Interim Three with a screech of blue static. First to swing up was a youngwoman: shimmer hosen, pin-heels, supermaze carrier. Epitome of sex and decency. Next a youngman: extensor, shin pads, inalienable cod. Four youngwomen, jiggle-suited, jump-booted. Finally an Ack Ack, white ackademickal open in a swirl, purple windmill proclaiming an unquestionable from the central booster.

The youngwoman put the carrier on the seat beside her, removing a catalogue of well-being manifests: "Equalops – surgery for gender parity", "Womb surrender and female freedom", "Womb banks, sperm banks, fair shares for free citizens". The youngman made to sit beside her. She lifted the carrier onto her knee, engrossed in "No more nasty menses". The four youngwomen bounded aboard, springs in their heels. A pretty sight in their pretty suits, playing at standing unsupported on the floor of the racketing gazibus. The Ack stayed by the door, wrapped his ackademickal protectively around him, mind on weighty matters.

The youngman removed his hand from the shaft of

his extensor and laid it on his knee. The youngwoman turned a page. He spread his legs, shin to her shin, weight shifted toward her. She edged away, replaced "No More Nasty Menses", brought out "Womb Surrender". He stretched, yawned, left his arm on the back of the seat, hand over the youngwoman's shoulder. She bent forward. He put his hand on her knee. She jerked, dusted it off with a catalogue. He gazed about him. Only an Ack Ack staring into the waves, dreaming of power and harnesses. Only a gaggle of jigglers, smoothing stomach pleats, offering gay abandon. He put his hand on her thigh.

Ithaca was wrapped, coated, in thought. What would the new ordinances mean to Karlin? A scattering of over forties lingering too long the wrong side of death: the city shrugged. Rumours of vast armies, oldwomen lurking in every dustbin: the city would rise as one, obliterate the common enemy. The citizens were weaned on scarcity; unrationed youth was economic, egalitarian, only because old age was outlawed. Womb surrender had not been the sexual equaliser Ithaca intended. While it was certainly spreading like core meltdown from Ackademick to open market women, yet Tramontanes, least desirable breeders, were proving most resistant. Proof of female longevity would release righteous male fury onto the streets, peremptory demand for high priority to compensatory sex quotas.

Ithaca's self-protective mesmer was shedding. She sloughed it. Flicked back from the waves, felt a glance in her direction, looked to its source. She saw the hand, the thigh, the woman and the man. In one bound she could pick up that prime piece of manhood, him and his inalienable cod, toss them through the window into the bay, leaving a glass silhouette and a howling draught.

The youngwomen swayed with the speed of the zibus and some intoxicant of their own, moved through to the benches, began throwing a nail scissors into the air, chucking it across the aisle, catching it

with a click. Then a nail scissors and a paperknife;
then a nail scissors, a paper knife and a boot hook.
The three sharp metal objects whirled and spun in the
air, juggled in higher, wider circles, snatched just
before falling on the youngman. They were skilled,
the youngwomen, had not, yet, dropped anything
despite their apparent and wild inebriation.

The youngman slipped both hands back into the
shaft of his extensor. The youngwoman with the
carrier gathered her belongings, stood up and changed
sections. The youngman rose. The youngwomen
followed. The light flashed for Interim Two.

"My stop," said the youngman.

The youngwomen nodded. One of them pinged the
buzzer with a well-aimed scissors. The gazibus
screeched. The youngman swung down to the windi-
est interim in the hinterland, huddling in his extensor,
to await the next zibus two hours hence. A sudden
kick to the back of the knee propelled Ithaca out the
door in his wake. Just retribution for one who,
perceived as part of the problem, moves too late to
remedy it? Ithaca's muscles rippled in helpless frustra-
tion. She had a sick lover to get home to, an
oldwoman who might collapse at any moment.

Ithaca looked at the youngman, who remained
huddled and hostile. Were youngwomen curious what
youngmen said to each other when no woman was
present? She could have told them. Nothing, looking
at the mountain wall; nothing, looking at the distant
waves; nothing, looking at the empty interim. Without
women there is no conversation.

"Cancerous tumours," the youngman hurled hope-
fully after the zibus, confirming Ithaca's impression
that even women's backs are better than a man's face.

Ithaca paced the platform composing, as she paced,
justification for according low priority to high-male
sex-ratios. The youngman was carving his name on his
arm. The blood, dripping in tiny drops, reminded her
of the pattern in city streets. Always a messy puddle,
then smaller splodges, smaller, fading, stopping. Life

stories engraved on the pavements, like love hearts in the sand: eternal witness, till the next rain, the next wave. Without revealing her high office, there was nothing she could do to expedite her return to the city. Honourable out. She would not be the one to find Karlin's body.

Not only a citizen, but an Ack Ack. Not only a youngman, but an unquestionable. Not only an Ack Ack, an unquestionable, but the city Ideo Logician, of which there was only one and that one was Ithaca Benaccar, son of Benaccar, Status Six. It was the function of the Ideo to explain the complex workings of the city to the satisfaction of its citizens. His precise identity must remain hidden: against bribes, false witness, disbelief. One secret.

Another secret: not only is Ithaca a woman, she is a woman whose womb was not surrendered, as required in equalops professions to avoid wasteful leave for menstruation, gestation, parturition. She is a woman whose lifting, carrying muscles have been unbruised, unbroken by womb removal. She is a woman who can heave a hundred kilos. Hurl a hundred kilos. Not only is Ithaca not the son of, she is not the daughter of Benaccar, Status Six. E'thane the Tramontane is Ithaca's mother. Not mother-hatch, not mother-vessel: her mother, who carried her and her brother for nine months in her own body, gave birth between her legs in pain and blood. Ithaca and Athos were born outside the city, brought to the Benaccar compound seven days old by E'thane the new nursemaid. But E'thane did not passively rear two more assimilated citizens. She taught her children the Tramontane heritage. They brewed ' and toasted in the ancient way, knowing never to say its name aloud, for ' meant life and, as E'thane explained, the name of the city meant death. When she met Zay, Ithaca could hear E'thane mocking, "Calls herself Tramontane. Where's her apostrophe? Closed up the letters to squeeze the Tramontane out." But Ithaca was not I'thaca, nor her brother A'thos.

So Ithaca paced. Neither male nor female, nor citizen nor zurban, and this two hour wait was neither blessing nor blame. She, whose job it was to force meaning, could make no symbol here. Everything was specific, nothing stood for anything else, and that is life, the gap life slips through.

Ninth Sighting: QUANTUM L.

On the stone benches of Observatory Walk sat a line of little nellies applauding their zapper brothers. It was cold: rousing cheers and hearty handclaps warmed the muscles, permitting icy bottoms to be removed from icy slabs shaken up and jiggled before repositioning. The delicate manoeuvres required of youngmen were hard to master; the little nellies were patient and encouraging, awaiting their turn. As one, soft, reedy zapper was, once more, knocked off balance in the knees-apart-strut, the devoted attention of at least one little nelly faltered.

"Feet apart. Knees bend. Elbows out. Hands in pockets. Strut. Strut, I said, not mince. Leave that to the nellies." Laughter. "Your mother-hatch stinted your shoulders so swing, swell, stride, compensate."

They could all have rehearsed in their sleep. Many did.

The daffy zapper was not Scimitel's assigned. Probably safe to roam the eyes, ears tuned for any breach in drill. Across the perimeter fence a long, sleek Quantum Libet pulled up smoothly at the crossway. No screech of brakes, no premature revs: driven like a youngwoman. Yet the covered head and padded arms bespoke a youngman. Nor was this some whipper zapper out in father's car. Scimitel glanced back quickly to the parade in case her attention had been missed. It was 'Opening the Twenty Twenty in a Crowd', knees spread assertively, elbows jabbed into ribs.

"Now nellies, over to you. Pad some peace between these warring zaps."

A city of scarce resources requires of its inhabitants a jigsaw fit: the antagonistic harmony of the parts which perfects the harmony of the whole. A muscle flexes, another will stretch: without either, the limb fails to function. Zappers stride and nellies trot, the different pace permitting staggered use of walkways. Youngmen it behoves to barrow and billow; demure youngwomen, elbows in, knees crossed, provide necessary space for a thrusting strut. First principles of concavity and convexity.

Scimitel Ekkos stole another glance at the driver of the Quantum. The car was moving, signalling left. No youngman signalled left. Where was the point? He had priority over the rear, and priority was all. But, dress codes? Youngwomen should not deprive a hardpressed city of the free pleasure of flowing hair or screw curls. Thin garments showed off the angles of a figure; folds of hefty fabric could so easily be taken for fat. The driver's padding might be organic: uncorrected flab, but a woman in a quantum? Scimitel was too old a little nellie to fail sex differentials. She should concentrate on drill; second nature was not enough.

The zappers pulled off extensors and shoulder pads; the nellies donned hobble shifts and pencil heels. Scimitel was absorbed in inhaling, squeezing ('Tight as you can get into. That's the way. They'll stretch. You don't want to.'), smiling and running with knees together, shins describing half circles, thigh touching thigh. The Walk was roped to allow two lanes for zapper practice. Unrealistic and unkind to expect zaps to hang around too long in the cold. Only made them hypercritical, which benefitted no one. Scimitel was moved over to the farthest lane for retrieval exercises:

one nelly drops a pin, which the other must pick up without losing her decency.

Scimitel's O-rays showed latent adipose surfeit. While at sixty six seasons her ribcage resembled a toast rack, yet without corrective action her eighty fifth would watch her outgrow the largest young-women's size. Scimitel must take the lifelong dark green leafy option. She attended weigh-in every twelfth, showing no sign of gain, but, as the machine pinged out cheerfully: "the uncontrolled appetite is the festering ground of the oboe". Knowledge of the potential for disgrace hidden in her skimpy frame made Scimitel reserved and cautious. She was growing a time bomb. When she stooped for the pin, her motions were spare and dry.

"No. No. No. Give us a good time. We know you won't lose your decency, but we like to be shocked."

The educator's voice boomed across the tracks. Scimitel bent again, striving to introduce a flourish, but lost sight of the pin. The Quantum had stopped short in a side street, caught in the corner of Scimitel's eye. The nellies and the zappers and the educator were all staring at Scimitel. Scimitel was staring at the car. Cancerous Duodetch, stalled on the highway. Tried a three point, got jammed, panicked. Wedged fender to fender, electric short. No use the Quantum backing, this was the only slipway to the northbound conduit for quarters around. Ithaca swung out and walked toward the smaller vehicle. How you could get stuck in a detch – the archetypal nelly-wagon. Ithaca surveyed the detch: position, angle, weight, volts. She strode to the steering side. The driver pressed the window switch.

"I'm so sorry. How silly of me. In this little car, to get stuck, such an idiot. Father traded for it but I'm quite hopeless. Below minimum voltage for the conduit only I couldn't face backing."

The driver saw an angry youngman in front of her, whose rightful highway she was blocking. Ithaca swallowed. At night she strode like a man, for her own safety, only to hear the scurrying steps of a youngwoman in front, trying to get away from her.

"Get out," she rasped, "I'll move it." Too public to risk disclosure. The driver scuttled.

Ithaca braced, grasped the front axle and lifted the carbody to the ridge of the road. She heaved the rear out similarly, reconnecting to the central booster.

"Oh my, oh my," the youngwoman gushed, "When you said 'move' I naturally thought . . . oh my, you are . . . what can I do to . . . do to? . . . "

Ithaca was back in the Quantum. The Duodetch sparked and drove off.

"Miracles of Manhood," proclaimed the educator.

Scimitel stared. It was a woman. A woman. A woman. She shouted silently round the square; her cry echoed and crescendoed off the cold glass fronts of the buildings, trapped and spiralling. Women can lift cars. Scimitel smiled, a lovely, open, expansive, relaxed smile of joy.

"Better," said the educator, "Much better. You can do it when you want to, Scimitel Ekkos. You can all do it when you want."

Tenth Sighting: BULLDOZER RISING

Outside the revolving door of Karlin's block had been placed a two-ton city skip, to be filled with the rubbish generated by a streetful of conscientious young homemakers. The lavish glee of purchase is surpassed only by the economic glee of disposal. Ithaca fitted her massive shoulder to the side of the skip, eased the metal hulk out of its moorings, parked the quantum in the resultant void.

Soren, rinsing soiled sheets in icy water, heard the grate and grind of the skip, announced to Essa,

"Ithaca."

Where is Ithaca now? She never leaves Karlin's side, watching the oldwoman's fingers stir softly on the blankets, knowing then that, at least, her lover is still alive. How very small is that 'least'. Did Ithaca hope that illness would kindle those tender feelings in Karlin which had so far remained dormant? Death seals unaltered; only life can change. Caring for Karlin seems despairingly like a holding action. It is difficult to believe, even for the old themselves, that age is not in itself a life-threatening disease. Ithaca slots herself into the rota Soren has called, finds even that intimacy she did share with her lover is eroded, as all who care for Karlin move into awkward equidistance.

Only when others must take over is the full richness of a human life laid bare: collecting food; cleaning, preparing food; feeding the mouth in mustardspoonfuls, placing a straw between cracked lips; holding the head up so the throat can swallow, holding the head up so the stomach can vomit, lifting the body for defecation; cleaning bed linen, cleaning the bedroom, cleaning the body; beginning again. While whoever was on rota must remove Karlin's muffling layers, check her body carefully for bedsores, unseen bruises, turn her every few hours to keep the blood flowing, oil dry skin, massage wasting muscles, only Ithaca appears naked before Karlin. She clings to this last vestige of reciprocity. Though Karlin's nakedness is enforced.

"Got other concerns now," mutters Essa, "than brutebrat's gorgeous youth."

The rota turns inexorably. One cleans out the cupboards, rearranges shelves to match her kitchen at home. Another removes the carpets in the corridor, "so that Karlin doesn't slip". Karlin is unlikely to slip, she is unable to get out of bed. But the woman disapproves of carpets, and so they must go. Another feels that the towels of an invalid should not be kept in the bathroom, they will only get damp. She puts the towels tidily away in the linen closet. When Karlin asks Soren for a towel, she does not know where to tell her to feel for one, and Soren needs precise directions. Is Karlin's mind wandering?

The women treat Karlin as they would treat themselves; they make of her their creature. They know what she should eat, how much, and when. They know whether she should have the window closed or the light off. They know when she should have visitors: they themselves are always welcome and, besides, they have replaced the onion lock with a keyhole, to which only they have keys. Security conscious. It is impossible that Karlin have wishes of her own which cannot be overridden "for health's sake". And yet without the love of these good women, Karlin would die.

Sometimes Ithaca wants to scream at the grey, withered figure immobile in the bed, "Where is Karlin? What have you done with the beautiful Karlin, you hideous old bag?" Sometimes Ithaca wants to dress up in her finest clothes, bend gently over the bed and invite Karlin, "Let me take you out to dinner, darling. I know you have to be sick, but couldn't you have a break this evening? I'll drive you in the Quantum."

Essa prepares nourishing, tasty meals which Karlin refuses. Essa knows they are tasty because they are just what she would like herself.

"Karlin's mind is wandering," Essa tells Soren.

Ithaca sits in Karlin's room, half-naked, and reads her poems about death. Often Soren recites from memory. It is what Karlin wants at last. She has favourites. Ithaca and Soren cry as they read, or recite; they are exhausted long before Karlin is sated. She always had more stamina.

"Ithaca is a bad influence," Essa tells Soren. She holds the poetry book in her hands, damningly open. "She makes Karlin think of death."

"Ithaca has no idea about illness," says Essa, "She does not let Karlin rest."

Soren likes Ithaca more now, likes the attention she pays Karlin, is relieved to note that Karlin is less involved than Ithaca. But Ithaca's youth is a problem. At any moment, if Essa made her angry, if Karlin made her miserable, if fatigue made her snappy, she could turn them all in. Soren can not endanger the Senectity for a kind manner and pleasing voice.

Ithaca felt more alone now than at any time in her ambiguous, androgynous, high-credit life. Maybe she had simply forgotten the others. Each flicker of community had been dashed by the demands of mobility. She had been a Tramontane, she had had a brother: both gone. She had had an adoring and indulgent father-possessor: he had left nothing but his high office. She had loved Zay, she had loved Karlin: Zay was lost, Karlin going, if ever she had truly been there for Ithaca. When she sat on Karlin's bed, holding her hand, partnering Soren in verses of poetry, Ithaca felt at the same time, community, at the same time, loss.

She was surrounded by oldwomen, more than she had ever seen before, and at such close quarters. Such poor, weak, limping bundles. Not like Karlin, who was beautiful, did not show her age, though presently shrouded in that tight, grey mask, under which she was all but unrecognisable. Ithaca watched Soren bumping her way along the corridor, graceless, blind fingers stabbing bluntly at empty space; Essa, leaning so heavily on the wall, body rocking with each step, and, Ideo Logician though she was, she felt she had hit rock bottom. Often she marvelled at such will to live. Would she wish to continue a life so ugly? Ithaca worried about the work she was not doing, the piles of ordinances awaiting justification. She worried about the proposed compensatory sex quotas and hygienic disposal measures. She should be preparing counters, though, hitherto, she had found the proposals an amusing logic ground. If the turnabout was for Karlin, and Karlin died, what did Ithaca owe Karlin's friends? Ithaca was unused to personal debt.

"Karlin," said Soren, "Your young friend is a danger to us."

"Yes," said Karlin.

"If we make her angry she can kill us," said Soren.

"Yes," said Karlin.

"We must get rid of her."

"No," said Karlin.

"You must send her away," said Soren.

"No."

Soren felt the bulldozer rising: Karlin must understand the danger, her responsibility. Was Essa right? Was Karlin's mind wandering? A light touch brushed Soren's clenched, impassioned fist, a feather from the duvet almost, or the top knuckle of a limp but determined hand. A gesture which packed: you insult my intelligence; you always were too hasty; and give

50

me time to speak, it costs such effort.

"Scrub," Karlin exhaled. Then, "Help," and finally, "Hero."

Eleventh Sighting: NAKED HEEL

"Business?"

"Return this book."

"On the desk."

"Only a couple of minutes. Save your legs."

The duty beadle at the welcome desk in the entrance hall of the Benaccar residence looked across to the new water closet and felt seasick.

"Give you five," he said.

Zay was already at the closet door. She stepped aboard, pressed the flush, admired the smooth speed with which the surge of water floated her up the building, the engineering which could withstand the weight and almost constant flux. Every sunset crowds gathered outside the residence to watch the water bubble up the lift shaft, the glass so transparently clean only the abrupt smack of pink ripples hitting the side showed how the liquid column was held in place.

At mezzanine five Zay skated out, picked her way over the prostrated Tramontanes (courtesy required that the host's head remain lower than the guest's) and approached the sanctum. Any last trace of Ithaca which might have lingered in library, bed or board-room had by now been wiped out by the clean, impassive sweep of the household Tramontanes. But there was, in the polished mirrors, the spotless titles, an air of waiting, as though the owner might yet be expected. There had been no clearance. Respectful silence? Homesafe was, sometimes, the last to hear of a burnout.

Strict instruction, coupled presumably with strict punishment, had prevented anyone from touching Ithaca's study. Fine dust had accumulated on the ordinator. Zay initialled it. How long before this 'Z' would, in turn, be covered over? Perhaps the oil in her fingertips would preserve it, a little. Grey streaks flashed up and down the screen, tuned to no particular programme, passive or active. Manifests, newspapers, even books lay open in piles, some dovetailed together. The rubbish bins had not been emptied in ages, a separate filing system in themselves; computer scree spilled over in long black coils. The wall monitor flickered out its tireless two part message:

HIGH-MALE SEX QUOTAS: LOW PRIORITY   JUSTI-
FICATION AWAITED
HIGH-MALE SEX QUOTAS: LOW PRIORITY   JUSTI-
FICATION AWAITED

No one but an unquestionable is called upon to justify. Zay stared with the mesmerised fear of one who sees something she does not want to know; whose knowledge, spoken or unspoken, will endanger her remaining days though she but vaguely understand what she sees; whose mind will continue to probe an answer, quietly in odd moments, though everything clamours that understanding is destruction.

This was a trap; the atlas bait. The door of the study remained softly ajar; no one came swooping down with pain and manacles. Bitter irony filled her: she was a Tramontane, therefore she could not read. A book in her hands, openly declared at the welcome desk, bespoke not a scholar, but a servant; her eagerness to get upstairs nothing more sinister than the desire to dawdle and joyride. She was as safe with their secrets as any of that illiterate herd who scrubbed and hosed for the city. Defiant, she faced the screen once more. They were half right: she could not tell what the two-part message meant.

Zay's five minutes were up. On the corner viewer the duty beadle was pointing urgently at a clock. Fearing he spoke to her, she panned the viewer to take in the length of the hall. A Benaccar Tramontane slunk in.

"You're late. Wasting my life waiting," snapped the duty beadle.

"Left you ten aphros, half tin joyjoy, lip smacking new . . ."

Zay switched the sound off on the ensuing argument. He'd forgotten her. She was that unimportant? Good. Zay shut the door firmly and began the search for Ithaca.

She found her everywhere: sober, cynical, even, occasionally, gleeful. Zay pulled a length of scree from the rubbish, held it to the light, read along at random.

THE UNCONTROLLED APPETITE IS THE FESTERING
GROUND OF THE OBOE
YOUNG WOMEN SHOULD NOT DEPRIVE A HARD-
PRESSED CITY OF THE FREE PLEASURE OF FLOWING
HAIR

Truisms every citlet learned from hatch, every assimilatory Tramontane must get word perfect, reinforced daily in the papers, on the hoardings. Zay thought she recognised the last reinforcement, a recent headline:

KERB CRAWLERS CURBED/TAKE YOUR FILL AT THE
CROSSROADS

Ithaca. Once, many seasons ago, after Zay had unwrapped the bindings from Ithaca's body, confirmed what she'd long hoped, expressed not horror, but delight for the sex revealed, Ithaca had made the ancient toast. Ithaca. Once, scraping a naked heel along the soft sand of the foreshore in the hinterland, she had written her own name, "I'thaca", then "Z'ay", with a love heart connecting the two. The next wave wiped them out, but not the knowledge that Ithaca lurked miles beneath her own surface. Ithaca.

Ithaca was not in any danger, nor any evident penury, had traded the zurban atlas because it was worse than useless. The city archives, pasted along the travelator, showed only too clearly what was left of whatever might once have flourished without its walls. The ceaseless, clamorous influx of female Tramontanes was living testament to the poverty of zurban life. Zay's impulse to trade for the book was itself suspect, weak nostalgic curiosity for a community long outgrown.

What had Ithaca thought of her? Clumsily Zay punched out "Tramontane" on the keys. Words spilled so fast across the screen that she had to slow the distributor.

TRAMONTANES EARN LESS BECAUSE THEY ARE WORTHLESS

Another mnemonic jingle. Why did Ithaca have all this received knowledge cluttering her ordinator? She was so contemptuous of her fellow citizens' need to learn by rote, a saying for all seasons. Zay pressed 'edit', meaning to alter the slogan so Ithaca would know she had been there. Before she could add any message of her own, the screen filled:

TRAMONTANES ARE EARNEST BECAUSE THEY ARE HONEST (!)
SLOWLY SLOWLY GOES THE TRAM AND LOWLY LOWLY STOOPS
TRAMONTANE BANE WANE DRAIN . . . SHAME
ULTRAMONTANE OUTSIDER SIMPLE AS NELLIES LOYAL DOCILE
TRAMONTANES ARE THE BANE OF EXISTENCE BUT OH WE LOVE THEM ALL THE SAME

Zay was shocked. There was no mistaking the last line. These were Ithaca's musings, her notes, perhaps, toward the final slogan. Zay turned abruptly and stared at the wall monitor. That was what she had seen before and refused to acknowledge: the transmission light was on. This was not 'received' knowledge for

Ithaca, it was all her own work. She rated, she prioritised, she justified. It was Ithaca who doomed Tramontanes to discrimination or assimilation, that lying sop to an easily pacified citizenry.

For a moment Zay shared the fury of baskets, oboes, nellies, sickies: all the second class citizens it was Ithaca's life work to justify. Zay touched the printout, its heat sensitivity was still partially active. Ithaca may only have been gone a twelfth. Zurban atlas still firmly clasped under one arm, Zay plucked a light bulb from the desk lamp and left.

Twelfth Sighting: TALL BIG STRONG

Scimitel Ekkos calculates: if only she can remain thin and tiny, the time will come slower when the words are said:

"She'll be beautiful when she's older."

"She's beautiful now."

When she will be taken from her citlet homesafe and given to the friend of her father-possessor. When she will hear the smacking of lips, feel the hot saliva and the rough tongue; when she, like countless nellies and zappers before her, will be eaten alive. "Licking" they say for nellies, "sucking" for zappers, but Scimitel has seen other nellies from her brood. She knows what she knows. She must take care to remain small and unremarkable.

Scimitel Ekkos calculates: if she can only grow tall big strong, like the youngwoman in the quantum, she will be able to lift cars, stalk the streets, wreak revenge. She must take care to eat up all the food on her plate, accept any overs going.

One night, as Scimitel loosened the silk cord between her ankles: short steps a shortcut to womanhood, she rubbed the knot against an inevitable bruise, winced, and jerked her head away to distract the pain. In the fluorescence of early evening a sleek metal body loomed beyond the street window.

"Scimitel Ekkos," called the driver of the quantum, "Here is a weapon. Tonight you are invulnerable. You can walk through the streets, through the park, through the homesafes and residences without interception. You can kill who you want."

Scimitel reached out a thin blue arm, took the weapon. An extensor, shin pads, inalienable cod: the full set of youngman's apparel. Nellies dressed their brothers for zapper practice, scrubbed the garments afterwards, stretched the cod back into shape, stitched and invisibly mended. The apparel was as familiar to Scimitel as her own, though she had never, save in secret jest with sister nellies, in the closed darning room, felt herself on the inside of its protective folds.

Scimitel finished unbinding her ankles, smoothed cool cream into the welts, tiptoed to the spyhole. The father-possessor (father, as they called him) liked to look in on his brood unobserved: in hot weather young limbs were often exposed above bedclothes. The innocent curve of a buttock, the smooth skin of a sleeping thigh might stir his manhood into physical possession. He had, however, borne over a hundred citlets; Scimitel might well huddle in obscurity a few more seasons.

Some citizens, glimpsed once at a distance, seem to shout at the top of breaking voices, with broken lungs, that obscurity is their only chance. Their awkward, hunched shoulders, their veins too near the surface, the fear in their own eyes declare that no good will come to them. When a man gets his natural urges in the vicinity, they are the ones to be caught, unless, by some chance, they are in bed that day with one of their recurring bouts of malediction. In their gait a stumble, in their face a loser's look.

Scimitel raised her glass to the spyhole, reversing the magnification, allowing her to see into the dayhall. Empty. But the meter was clicking. Someone was awake and using more than background voltage. Scimitel counted: more than side lamps, less than a heater. Sound simulator? No sound. Personal closed circuit. Perfect. Uncannily like a piece of luck. Maybe the weapon was already working. She returned to the window, opened it the full seven and a half inches, just below the radar alarm, affording her small head a quarter inch clearance.

In the protective shadow of the outer wall, Scimitel donned the weapon. The extensor was enormous, enveloped her finger tips, covered the shin pads. She trembled for the fraud she was committing; she could never bring it off. In a hopeless gesture she strapped on the inalienable cod, punishing her ludicrous audacity. Bright green, even in the gloom. Voices approached. Scimitel turned to the wall as if to urinate, zapper drill second nature, she had watched so often. The voices passed. It was true. She was invulnerable. Who would she kill?

Some citizens should not trust to luck, should view 'good fortune' as a snare. Does Scimitel believe Ithaca's power lies only in her clothes? Does she think youngmen are not attacked alone at night? Why does she not stay homesafe, dreaming of the man who will call her beautiful? Silly little nelly with the skinny arms and frightened eyes.

Scimitel made for the wall of the residence, scrabbled against it, extensor sleeves flapping round her handholds, shin pads heavy on her legs. Her shoes slid helpless off the slippery glass; each time she gained ground, it was pulled from under her. Scimitel sat down and gazed at the shiny mountain with its sheer, vertical sides. She was so small, the wall so big. But everything is big when you are small, and everything gets smaller when you look, made up of tiny things. Scimitel unknotted her shoe laces, the soles of her feet, tuned to the irregularities of flooring in her homesafe, where any creak calls attention, would stroke a passageway up the glass on the slightest curves. She tied her laces together, wondered where to strap them for the ascent. The inalienable cod stuck out, redundant, it would push her away from the wall which she needed to hug closely. Impatiently she hung the shoes over it, tugged it round to the back.

The wall, when no one was yelling "Faster. Faster. If you can't, stand aside for those who can," was not smooth, but pitted and cracked, curling here outward, there in. It would not take the weight, or the toe, of a larger body, but Scimitel picked her way up, the cold rounded glass pressed close to her rejoicing cheek. Footsteps too light to open automatic doors; arms, aching at full stretch, too short to grip the ceiling strap on the travelator; head too low to purchase at the Supermaze counter, yet only she, the delicate Scimitel, could scale the slippery glass.

A yard from the top, she stopped. The swirls had slowly given way to a vertical, impassive surface as sheer, and impossible to climb as the window of the day-hall. Two moments hesitation, while she eyed the crown of metal spikes which stuck up like a zapper haircut into the sky. Then she leapt. A dandelion puff, more likely blown away in the breeze than held down by gravity. Mid-air was terrifying; landing solid, hands round firm steel, was a triumph. The sweet taste of physical triumph. Tempted to slide back down again just for the pleasure of that leap. If you parted your legs, in a most indecent fashion, and distributed your weight evenly on each side, feet wedged neatly between metal spikes, you could stand on the top of a high wall, possessor of the city, without fear of overbalancing. Discoveries. Joy in zapper secrets. In shin pads no one could peer up your hobble skirt.

Over the other side, no hooks snapping, skirts riding, no future breasts to keep from joggling: Scimitel ran.

Thirteenth Sighting: LIGHT BULB IN A
BURN-OUT PARK

Bundled up in clothing three sizes too big, a small, twig-like figure came thudding down the street. As though a shivering whippet borrowed the fleece of a Saint Bernard to ford the stepping stones of a stream. The extra weight is sure to upset that delicate balance and throw its wearer into cold, rushing water. Scimitel, half-flying in her speed, stumbles in the shin pads, feels her ankle buckle, finds her face a sudden half inch from the sparkling roughness of the pavement. At first she gazes calmly at the quartz glints in the stone. Then she realises the glory of shin pads which, when oversize, might trip, but also cushion the fall. She swayed to her feet, let herself drop once more to the ground; again, again, till her legs knew the simple folds necessary: ankle, knee, hip which make of accident a game.

Scimitel began to feel more at ease outside on the street alone than tucked up in her own homesafe. Figures walked by hurriedly, bent to their own destination. Fellow citizens leant against railings passing around white joyjoy with an air of sluggish generosity. Smiling beatifically, one offered the tin to Scimitel. Joyjoy still made her cough, and the bitter taste always stained her throat. Before clumsiness gave her away, another joyrider took the tin.

"No lacklust intended," Scimitel apologised banally.

"None taken," came the reply, and the joyjoy continued on its peaceful semi-circle.

A properly educated nelly is conversant with all kinds of hallucinogens, aphrodisiacs, stimulants and depressants. Joyjoy is definitely a depressant, passé and, some would say, even, soporific. Who would waste their market hours inducing sleep, temporary paralysis of the nervous system, which most sensible citizens were doing their best to excite? Scimitel walked on, engrossed in the citizenly gaggles crowding off the pavement, largely ignorant of the social context of her refusal. She did not see the empty tin of joyjoy whizz past the back of her head, its jagged lid missing her ear by a fine hair. She did not hear the hurled insult.

"Crawl back into father's mouth, slimey little slug."

Already seven, no eight, youngmen had looked her in the eye and Scimitel had smiled back man to man, but without patting her inalienable. Zapper signals worked so smoothly. Nellies could never be too careful: "Enigma fascinates. Ambiguity frustrates." Scimitel must forget any unfortunate nelliedom still lingering about her, concentrate on zapping. Not till she had strode her short-legged way through the open market to the beginning of the Ackademick zone, did she think again about killing.

The burn-out park, across a six-lane highway, looked a calm place to think. Scimitel tried out the push buttons on the crossway: like model cars upon a model roadway, each driver slowed and stopped. She was not even a protected unit in a citlet crocodile. Male apparel was a wondrous thing. Such civic admiration, and no one to commend her for it. Did Scimitel herself remember how she had learned what to admire?

In the quiet, traffic-punctured twilight of the burn-out park, she listed her enemies. Father-possessor, most often glimpsed licking his lips in the distance, but ever-present with his cameras, his two-ways, the talk of nocturnal visits. First target. Educator, who made her practice smiling under all conditions. Dietician, who measured her wrists and ankles with a thumb and forefinger, and the invariable diagnosis, "latent, latent". The zaps who tormented her because she was small, who told tales when she snapped her ankle bands running away. Yes, but more; there must be more to kill than that.

From the ceiling of the crematorium hung an enormous cut glass ball, turning slowly, shooting sparks of red blue white. Both source and reflection of light. Without the original source, there would be no later reflection. Someone had thought it all up. Someone had decided that nellies kept their knees together, made the zappers' beds for them. It wasn't right. Zappers took advantage of having a nelly in their room, attempted your decency, and when they succeeded it didn't count, because with zappers it was only practice. "Don't make such a fuss. It doesn't count. Only your pride's hurt. Your decency's intact." But it did hurt. Sometimes it bled.

So which first? Did someone decide who should do what, then everybody did it? Or did everyone behave how they thought, then someone said what they were doing was how things ought to be?

Someone was coming. Scimitel strained to see. A tall figure swooped across the highway, skates glinting as it rounded the corner into the burn-out park. It headed straight for the high kerb, only at the last minute pulling its knees up to its chin, springing into the air. Around its neck was a bag containing some light object. It did not notice Scimitel sitting quietly on her bench, but sped toward a newly dug flower bed, whose grey soil attested the recent recycling of human ashes. The skater kneeled, with the sudden comic clumsiness of a penguin landing on an ice floe, stark contrast to its previous grace. At the end of a row of freshly planted bulbs the skater began scraping carefully at the earth. From the bag at her neck she took a light bulb, half buried it in the ground. Then she jumped back from knees to wheels and spun off out of the park.

Scimitel gaped. The city at night, subject of so many stories and terror-warnings, amazed her with its mild darkness, its glowing lights, out of which appeared these unlikely citizens. A light bulb in a burn-out park: last tribute to a lost friend? a practical pun? a private joke? Scimitel did not want to waste time killing, she could do that any day. She would not use up the weapon scratching old scabs.

Fourteenth Sighting: FOOTSTOOLS OF THE ACKADEMY

For more years than she cared to remember, Malachi Lorluss had been updating codot. Three hundred seasons. She remembered. She did not choose to remember. She was burdened with a memory which allowed her to forget nothing. The day she got stuck in the staff turnstile was the day she broke the cane chair in the filing cabinet was the day she weighed in at two hundred pounds was her twelfth birthday was the day she started work was forty years ago.

"The turnstile is the perfect gateway. It screens out the unfit: the old, the sick, the short and the obese, those who are not fit to enter the Ackademy."

As the only part of her which felt full was her power to recall, she at first concluded that the weight problem was caused by an overactive memory gland, consequently cut memorable activity to a minimum, lived a strict and arid routine. At two hundred pounds choice was limited. She could offer her thighs to such as prefer flesh obese, or she could rot. She chose to rot. Instead she got fatter. Fat like the new moon. Fat like a tidal wave. She spread everywhere. Every day of every season, dark, cold, flood, light, hot and dry, Malachi Lorluss, at three hundred pounds, had blocked the southbound travelator, held up the crowds on the central concourse, slowed all movement to a trickle while she fitted an onion skin to a small concavity in the shiny tiles and entered the footstools.

The trade tunnel of the footstools of the Ackademy was wide and empty one minute, wide and roaring the next as trolleys rattled past on metal tracks, turning a sharp L bend, disappearing into the guts and tubes of the lower levels. Malachi scrutinised their human load for wriggle or squirm of resistance. The Scrub accepted for recycling only those derelicts who lifted their little fingers. Often there was no stir: so many wrecks abandoned hope, and derailments remained unsuspiciously infrequent. That an oboe should loom up on the tracks, interpose her body between the roaring trolley and the ether slabs of the Ackademy, did not feature in even the wildest dreams of impossible rescue. The broken heaps of aged, sickly and crippled citizens, rounded up for magnetic scanning, seldom recognised a miracle when they saw her. Few trolley loads believed that theirs was a body worth surviving in. Though they came at dawn each day to whisk survivors off to a new life in the refugee camps of the Scrub, the Senectity found the waiting room empty, more often than not, and settled down instead to gossip with Malachi.

Now that she was old as well as fat, Malachi inhabited the tunnels, seldom venturing into the concourse, feeding on the offerings of fortune-seekers who came cloaked and nightly to hear what might befall them. Fortune-telling was as popular as it was outlawed; snatching pieces from the future tantamount to prolonging life. Malachi, updater of codes, knew before any open-market citizen what new ordinance would shortly regulate their days. Many seekers liked best to explore their present situation, accepting only that advice which confirmed their chosen path, advice which, recited endlessly to themselves, yet sounded magical from the mouth of another. Often all parties to a dilemma would visit, singly and clandestinely.

Then Malachi appeared a prophet, knowing each protagonist better than they knew themselves. Soren the scrupulous, found the activity immoral and what if the fortune-seekers caught sight or sound of survivors awaiting whisk off? What, Malachi countered, of the rich information the seekers unwittingly gave the Senectity? the precious gifts which supplemented meagre fare? Soren remained scrupulous; Malachi sophistical.

No survivors this morning, only three fortune-seekers booked in for the evening. Malachi settled down to codot. In the green metal cabinet a corridor of intrays surrounded and surmounted one small abacoid. Only the current, updated stage of the codot was held in the chips and coils of the processor, but all previous stages must be stored for reference in sandproof boxes, like last season's photographs of beloved offspring, no less a father's son for having been outgrown. No ordinance was retroactive, each citizen must situate their behaviour in reference to the ordinances prevailing on the day of action. Malachi spent her years filing amendments confirmations updates downgradings, matching justification to ordinance, no ordinance valid without justification, no ordinance respected without high priority. The tranceptor still bleated yesterday's question:

HIGH-MALE SEX QUOTAS: LOW PRIORITY?

Malachi filed the sex quotas 'pending'.

Ten years passed. Or ten hours. Time for the fortune-seekers.

"Displacement required: time, place or person?"

"I want to know what the future holds."

"Depends on the present, and your intentions."

Scimitel paused, shifted in her chair, still stiff from her night on the bench in the burn-out park.

"What's my father-possessor doing now?"

"I see a high wall, a crown of spikes at the top. The wall is made of glass, shiny and slippery."

"My homesafe," breathed Scimitel.

"The other side of the wall is a large, marble building; in front of the building stand two men talking."

"My father and my father's friend."

"They are talking about you. The younger man is saying . . . "

"No," cried Scimitel.

" . . .! She'll be beautiful when she's older!"

"And my father?" gasped Scimitel, "What does he reply?"

"He says, 'She's beautiful now.'"

"No," cried Scimitel again, "Look at me. Look at me, sitting in front of you. I'm not beautiful. It's a lie."

Malachi looked at the thin, pale seeker before her. She saw a dead white face, a face under water, white as worms kept underground, white as the eyes of deep sea fish, skin jerked tight over sharp bone, the only track of colour the blue throbbing veins at the temple. It spoke intelligence and suffering, which youngmen indeed called beautiful. Malachi shivered, put a surreptitious hand to her own fat thigh, grateful for the rich rolls of her own flesh. She must not lie, or she would forfeit her gift of fortunes.

"You are beautiful," she pronounced.

Scimitel sank. "I'm not going back," she said at last, "Show me what happens when I don't go back."

"I see a tall stranger," said Malachi.

"The driver of the Quantum?"

"None other."

"We were at drill when I first saw her. I thought she was a man. She lifted a detch right up in the air, turned it round, then put it down again reconnected. I nearly clapped. Last night she came to me."

"She asked you to follow her."

"Maybe. Maybe I didn't understand. She gave me these clothes."

Scimitel waved her straw arms in their weight of zapper raiment, soiled and crumpled. "I went on the streets by myself. It was exciting."

70

"You spent the night out."

"Yes."

"You follow the tall stranger, you have adventures," said Malachi, "but adventures are dangerous. You go home, you're safer, you live longer."

"You're not telling me anything."

"If you stay you will be eaten alive. If you go you will be swept out of your depths. You will save lives, you will be a hero. But I see a shadow, a cold, clutching shadow."

"I am not afraid of shadows," said Scimitel. "They hide me."

"Before I tell you where to find the gateway out of the city, what have you brought for my services?"

"I have nothing of my own, I have brought what I found." Scimitel put a light bulb on the table between them.

"Very useful, a light bulb." Malachi shook it. "Even a dead light bulb."

Scimitel smiled. Malachi turned the bulb over.

"I see you earthed it for me."

"It was planted in the burn-out park."

"Take the hanging gazibus to the hinterland. You will find the gateway at Interim Two."

"Displacement required?"

Ithaca pushed the metal cabinet away with her toe, more room for her legs.

"I have been sent on a dangerous mission. My lover is old and ill and, maybe, dying. Her friends have asked me to go into the Scrub, to fetch help, they think the women may know a cure. At first I was scared. I said one of the friends should go, since she knows the people and the place. But the friend is blind. She was angry with me. She said she would never get out of the city alive, let alone the Scrub, whereas I am young and strong and healthy."

"Someone is going with you."

"When my lover first got ill, I left a message. I had a

friend. We loved books together. I sold an old atlas for her to find, so she would know I needed her."

"She found it."

"Last night I passed the burn-out park where we used to read. She had buried a light bulb in one of the beds. It was a joke that only she would make, her sign that she had got my message and was coming after me. We always used the city as our telegraph."

Malachi must not lie or she would forfeit her gift of fortunes.

"You're wrong," she said. "You are no heroine on an errand of mercy. You have been sent away because you are a nuisance. Your lover cannot rest with you there. You cause friction among her friends. You are being asked to prove commitment by accepting slight discomfort."

"That's not true."

"The one you called for help, she means to kill you. She believes you are the cause of her worst humiliations."

"You lie."

"The light bulb she planted, did it look like this?" Malachi placed Scimitel's gift on the table between them.

"Like that, yes, and any other bulb from any of the sockets of any of the lights of the city. A cheap trick. You took that from your own reading lamp."

"And did I smear soil around it too?"

Ithaca dug her nails into the earth.

"You will leave the city. You will go to the Scrub, to the women, and you will bring back something of great worth. You will find companions to help you. If you can make them companions."

"How do I get there?"

"Before I tell you where the gateway stands, what have you brought for my services?"

"It is too large to bring in here," said Ithaca, "Though the tunnels are wide indeed. But here is the key to the quantum libet now parked on the roof of two detches in front of the staff turnstile."

Malachi put the key in her lining.

"Hanging gazibus to the hinterland. Get off at Interim Two."

"Displacement required?"

"Where is she?"

"Which?"

"The one responsible. The one who makes up reasons why everything wicked, wrong and unfair is really good, right and just."

"The one responsible and the one who makes up reasons are not the same one."

"I've seen her tapes and her print-outs. I know what she says about us. Why should she justify if she's not responsible?" Malachi released the shutter on the tranceptor, the lid sprung open revealing the screen and the question:

HIGH-MALE SEX QUOTAS: LOW PRIORITY?

"You don't fool me," snapped Zay, "You're a jumped-up filing clerk with last season's computer terminal. I'm sure every office in the city is hanging on her reply."

"As a setter places each letter in even lines, an equal or a double space from each contiguous letter, she justifies. She makes equality among the letters she is given. She does not choose the letters, she is not responsible for the words they form. Your simplicity calls the setter guilty, kills the setter: you do not discover who provided the letters."

"Where is the setter, the justifier?"

"Gone to the Scrub. Before I tell you where the gateway stands, what have you brought for my services?"

"I have only one thing of value," replied Zay, "I give you that." She placed a pair of silver skates upon the table between them.

"Hanging gazibus to Interim Two. The gateway is there."

"Displacement required?"

"Would that."

"Soren. I'm pleased to see you."

Malachi was always pleased to see Soren. Better still if Soren never left. What she saw in Essa Foujad, that bastion of rebellion and convention. Essa would bring back dictators for the pure pleasure of drawing moustaches on their photographs and sticking her tongue out. But Malachi knew wherein Essa's attraction lay. She wrapped Soren in accurate warmth, and the comfort in which Soren basked was more than physical. Essa provided the conservative stability from which Soren's radicalism could blaze forth secure and well-fed.

Malachi had news she knew would interest Soren, show the utility of telling fortunes.

"There's going to be trouble," she announced.

"What's new?" Soren shrugged.

Malachi related her three visits, concluding, "The city fathers have asked for high-male sex quotas. Seen too many of us around; don't think it's fair. The Ideo's given it low priority, but she's neglected to file her justification. I've made it 'pending', but they won't wait long. We'll have to find her." Soren gaped. Malachi was impressed, never sure of her own importance until Soren approved.

"You don't listen to what you're told. We've sent the Ideo away. You gave her the shortcut. She's a danger to the Senectity and a danger to Karlin," Soren snapped. She rested her forehead in her palm.

"How's it going?" asked Malachi.

"Worse. Worse worse worse worse and worse."

"Soren, I'm so sorry."

Malachi swallowed her awkwardness, pulled Soren toward her, rested the blind woman's head on her shoulder, and hugged her. Two fat oldwomen nestled together. As Malachi struggled to keep sex out of her mind she was caught up first in Soren's sobs, then in thoughts of Karlin. Then she cried for all remembered sadness and because there was comfort in hugging a warm fat body, and because that body was Soren's.

Fifteenth Sighting: RUTHLESS KILLERS

Scarcely able to speak, Karlin announced that everyone must go home now, she was tired of entertaining.
Indignant, or patient, the rota explained that she was
ill. Karlin pointed out that this was why she needed to
rest. The rota were concerned she would be unable to
manage alone. Karlin replied her needs were few,
bedbound as she was. The rota said they would worry
about her. Karlin said this was only natural, but
perhaps they could comfort each other.

Karlin was eroded by her inability to be herself. She
had thought she was more than a sum of voluntary
muscles. The less she recognised herself in the reactions
of her attendants, the closer she felt to the anonymity
of death. Only Ithaca made scant allowance for illness, but her constant presence had been constant
reproach. Brain alert in an inactive body, Karlin
assessed her chances. The rota could leave a day's
worth of such food and water as she might swallow
on the table beside her bed. When they came to wash
plates and replenish stock, they could help her to the
commode, she would need it no oftener. Liberation.
Ten free hours to concentrate on living.

Soren and Essa left with the others. Essa said they
gave in too easily. If you were ill, you went to the
hospital, après-ski as they called it nowadays. Soren

spoke of the hours spent saving survivors from magnetic leaching, the uses to which old and diseased bodies were often put, but she was tired. She would have liked a whole night's sleep, would have liked to entrust Karlin to the proper authorities, to believe in the propriety of authority.

"We're leaving her to die," Essa announced as she and Soren flopped like blown litter onto a garden wall.

"If that's what she wants."

"We should get Ithaca to take her to the après-ski. There must be something they can do."

"Kill her," said Soren. "We sent Ithaca to the Scrub."

"It's all wrong. Karlin needs proper treatment."

"I've known her almost as long as I've known myself. We have to do what she wants. She'll never get better on someone else's orders."

"Stubbornness. If you're such a good friend, why don't you do something for her?"

"I'm doing it."

Two discarded rubbish bags slumped on a low garden wall, full of broken glass and eggshells.

"Essa," Soren, conciliatory, broke the silence, "Neither of us has slept for a quarter, let's . . . "

"Sleep on it? And by morning the problem will have 'passed away'? Why don't you care, any of you in the Senectity, why don't you grow up? Autonomy, dignity – fatalism I call it."

"Essa, stop. I love Karlin."

"I hope you never get to love me in quite that way."

"Jealousy? You're incredible."

"You're enjoying it, Karlin's illness, being all important."

"Leave me alone."

If that's all you can say, if you don't care how much you hurt me, if you cannot offer warmth and softness, then, then you must go away and leave me alone.

Essa stood up and stumbled off. Soren sat. She had thought that at this time Essa was owed to her, that

76

lovers clung together more fiercely when death prowled. What monster would leave a blind old woman sitting alone at night on a brick wall? Essa was a monster. A jealous, cold, callous ... Or was Soren callous not to argue all night, if need be, with Karlin? Essa lived around the corner, Soren would bang on the door, tell her off, and by morning they would have made it up. But when she finally gathered herself to go, a picture of the streets and pavements she must walk ready in her mind, it was to Karlin's Soren directed herself.

"Soren?" sobbed a breathless voice, "Soren? First hours were bliss. Alone. But I needed commode. No strength. Frightened. Mess."

"It's okay. You're okay. I'll put you back in bed, then I'll clean you up."

"Hold me."

The smell was strong. How terrible to lie in your own dirt. Soren wrapped her arms round Karlin, shocked, despite herself, at the desperate thinness; there was so little to hold.

"Well?" asked Essa with the morning puree, "Will she go? If she won't go after all this you can cross me off the rota. I'm not being done for mirthless murder."

"They don't care, Essa. Why don't you know that? They want us off the face of their pretty young earth."

"I thought the Senectity was to protect us on the streets, but you make everyone under forty into ruthless killers."

Karlin slept. Soren listened to the voices of the young passing in the street.

"Six sugar loaves and a quarter ton of desiccated thrace. Should do for a day in the hinterland."

"Been before?"

"Always pays to overspend."

"By the time we return, we can sell it off for

double." Innocent merriment. How dare they, young and vicious, revel in their smug health when Karlin, who was good and clever, was so ill? Soren wished them dead, eaten by cancer within the year. Soren, tireless worker for the Senectity whose code-word was "Choose life", Soren was wishing death on two inoffensive strangers laughing in the street.

Karlin woke. A strange prickle, no a ripple, a tweak was happening along her left side. She lay a long while, wondering, exploring. Stretched flat, immobile in the dark, she realised what it was. The cotton wool was shredding, the barbed wire melting, sensation returning. After the initial plummet, when every anxious enquiry was greeted with the single, despairing answer, "worse", it seemed that Karlin was getting better. Had taken advantage of Essa's tiff with Soren, a temporary decoy, to sneak in a little improvement. As she began to feel her leg again, she was proud. She had done this. She had lain as still as she needed to, as quiet as she needed, she had worked hard, and she was better. The night ended in a wet, frightening mess, but Karlin knew she was right. You cannot judge an outcome by an ending.

Soren stood at the bedside. "Malachi's here. We're meeting at her place. Fresh water in the hole on your left, with a straw. Boiled kerris on the shelf, cold I'm afraid. Sure you'll be alright?" She wanted to get to the meeting. Wanted the night off. Didn't want to leave Karlin alone.

"No."

"Want to risk it?"

"Yes."

"How do you feel?"

Karlin's achievement was secret, mustn't be tampered with, or scared away. Karlin took pity on Soren.

"Better."

Sixteenth Sighting: HALL OF THE ABNORMALIDADS

She must do it herself then. Since everyone was against her. What pleasure in life to stand idle when someone needed you? Essa hurried through the awakening streets. Nearing mid-day, the early risers among the young were out of bed already, popping their first pill of the day, peeling their brains out of night head-phones. In sufficient time Essa spotted a youngman ahead: her impatient bustle slowed to a glacial crawl. Excruciating, given her present urgency. The youngman skimmed past, no more aware of her than of yesterday's headlines.

"Karlin," said Essa, "It's for your own good. They'll find out what's wrong and make you better. You want to get better. Wasting away here. Vomiting and not eating. Vomit blood next. When there's nothing else. And dehydrated. Don't drink enough to keep a blade of grass alive."

"I've made a bundle of your necessaries: towel, comb, soap. And I found a pink smock in my sewing basket. Make a better impression than those pyjamas. The car will be here in fifty minutes. Time to give you a good scrub. Appointment? Indeed not. You're an emergency. Go in style. Though we could have avoided the fuss and bother if you'd agreed to go last season. I'll just call them on the tube, check which entrance."

Within seconds the card returned.

"Car park full. No waiting. No standing. Dial 431 to book a parking meter."

"Oh really. I'll go myself on the travelator. Make them take you without a parking space. Used to be an Ack Ack, had a bit of clout. Not status six, like your young Ithaca. But a high up."

They shouldn't blame everything on the young. Too sweeping. We built a fine city. If things have gone wrong, that's our legacy, we must sort it out together. All that hope and freedom, they were a good basis. We planned these acres, same as the youngmen. Didn't put the plan into action, but it was before equalops and everyone had a lot to learn. They like to forget now, that they were part of it. Used up their share and want to outlive themselves. No wonder the young call us selfish. We must all get together, young and old alike, round a table.

Essa believed in tables.

The Après-Ski complex towered above the central concourse. Essa headed for the main gallery as though she held in her hand a red thread which unrolled before her. For thirty years she had inspected and innovated the conduits of the tower, its lay-out was in her blood. Young purposeful figures moved smooth and engrossed. Essa was proud of her design. Only the odd visitor, pausing to gaze at the floor plan, caused a little swirl in the straight flow of determination. The women crouched at the skirting boards, scrub in hand, were so evenly spaced that their successful navigation was easily choreographed into the swiftest stride.

The duty beadle at the welcome desk was busy. Quicker to go straight to the lying-in wards. First left. Second right. To the end of the corridor then . . . what stairs were these? Maybe a mezzanine. Essa sat a little minute on the bottom rung. No one was about. She clambered up the staircase, clinging more than a little to the guardrail. Another gallery. She was merely circling the welcome desk, better to go back there. This time the staircase seemed much shorter. Probably because she was going down. But the next level led to a huge archway. Tiring, Essa decided to enquire within. Over her head the arch announced:

"Hall of the Abnormalidads."

With a weary effort she pushed open two glass doors and, as the second swung closed behind her, a great, overpowering something threw itself upon her. It leapt unseen, attacking from all sides at once. Essa expected any moment to fall, crushed beneath its blows. Her tongue tasted of corpses, the thick slime of decomposition. Her nails scratched wildly at her skin. Worst of all was the stench the monster brought with it, so close it was in Essa's breath, like an exhalation from her own rotting stomach. No air in the hall, only this invasion. Essa could neither hear nor see through it. Not till she too had become incorporated did her other senses begin to function and she realised that the smell itself was the monster.

On either side of an aisle, stretching way back till a sudden right-angle interrupted the perspective, lay two rows of crisp white beds. Each bed was occupied by the decaying body of an oldwoman, each body wired to a machine, each machine gleaming the metallic gleam of surgical intervention. Whatever wounds were apparent, the presence of shiny metal testified that they had been executed with precision and were comfortingly medical. The machines themselves varied so much in shape, size and colour that at first they were a mere confusion of surfaces. Essa began a slow catalogue, attempting to isolate each in its own complexity. The first was a round chromium barrel whose only sign of life was the unconscious head protruding from its further end. The next, a giant octopus, clasped a female figure to its belly, steel tentacles inserted into every orifice. Gleaming wires held the hind quarters of the occupant of the third bed suspended from the ceiling. A fourth displayed a bloated arm with a hole in the wrist through which plastic tubes circulated a red liquid from one cannister to another. The rest of the body lay shrouded in a sheet. Without taking her eyes off a row of bubbles moving slowly and steadily up the tube toward the hole in the woman's wrist, Essa slumped backwards into a chair.

"Look away," hissed a voice so far down the aisle Essa could not see which of the living dead had spoken. The sudden command served, however, to sever her attention.

"Those the smell doesn't catch, the bubbles finish off," the voice continued. "What's the matter with you all? Never seen a woman die before?"

"She's not dead yet?"

"Is now. Lucky soul. They like to see how long a body can last with the bubbles marching on the heart. But it's the terror kills you. Strapped down like that, nothing you can do but feel them coming closer."

"Poison gas?"

"Pure oxygen. Only breath of fresh air in the hall."

Essa stared again at the oldwoman covered in the white sheet who had been alive.

"Look away. Or you'll take her place. Don't you wonder why there was a chair tucked so conveniently behind your knees when you felt a little faint?"

Essa moved down the hall toward the voice. In front of her stood an oldwoman wheeling a metal frame. From the crosspiece hung a bag of transparent fluid.

"You're one of them," said Essa.

"And you'll join us any minute less you keep your noise down."

"Why do they let you loose?"

"Don't know I can walk. First years I was so anaemic, with the blood letting, I could hardly shift. Surprising what you adapt to."

"What's the blood for?"

"I like to imagine some oldwoman is using it somewhere, bathing in it to keep her skin young; drinking it, maybe, to keep herself alive for another thousand years. But that's all folktales. They're using it for tests."

"Tests for what?"

"Research. Ackademic research. Medickal research. Have to keep their points up or they lose tenure. Then they're out on the open market."

"Where are they all now?" whispered Essa.

"The Acks are dictating their theories. The nurses are round the L bend, entertaining Patient Y. The Acks wired up her central nervous system so her reactions are unpredictable. She's conscious, but she has no control over her movements. They've put a high-pitch whine in her voice box. The nurses can't stand the noise. They hate her. In the evening, when all the dials have been checked and the graphs put to bed, the nurses get to play with Patient Y. They stick pins in the soles of her feet, the skin between her toes, her armpits. They place bets which part of her body will jerk, how long it will take her to respond."

One thought in Essa's head: escape, escape, escape. Get out of this place before a nurse should find her and, by some ghastly mistake, wire her up like those others.

"You're here on an errand of mercy. Friend needing urgent admission? Unconscious lover? Bleeding heart?"

"I have to go now."

"First you must help me."

"I can't."

"Quiet. Quick, under the bed."

Two nurses came swinging round the L bend, inspecting meters and gauges. At the bed of the oldwoman under the white sheet, blood still recycling between two cannisters, they stopped.

"Look at this one."

"Poor soul."

"I'm doing it tonight, Milo. Can't stand any more."

"Be careful. She's a great favourite, Patient Y. Lot of technology went into her."

"It's indecent. One shot of this to the heart and

she's out. They won't even notice she's gone."

"How can they bear it here?" asked Essa. "Those were human beings, those two. The stench would be enough. Surely."

"The young can't smell. Had you forgotten? Lucky you. The poppers and the aphros and the joyjoy and the chocolate chivers and the sugarfix. Those two are new. Seeps in slowly but they institutionalise fast. Staff spend longer here than the patients. They'll take a downer tonight. Patient Y's been murdered twenty times to my knowledge. She was dead when they brought her in here. It's the first thing the new ones try. First and last. Get resigned after that. Don't know who's dead and who's not, including themselves. The Acks built Patient Y to entertain the nurses, put them in the right frame of mind."

Essa swallowed. Felt some compassion returning.

"I'll help you," she said.

"Sit here. You're going to get this metal tube out of my arm. Bind my forearm with a tight bandage, stop the blood flowing. Cut round the tube till you can get a grip on it. It's in quite deep, the flesh is already growing over. Then sew up the wound."

"I'll faint. Can't stand the sight of blood."

"You won't faint. It's too important. Don't think about what you're doing. Just do what I tell you. Step by step. Soon you'll have done it and we can get out of here."

"But . . . if . . . Patient Y . . . is . . . already . . . dead . . . maybe you're all . . . maybe you are . . . maybe you're dead."

"I thought that. It's a risk. Or maybe I'll die when I come off the machine. But I've tasted the liquid in those tubes. It's water. Slightly salty water. Either way, this isn't life."

"How will I get you out? You'll be in a terrible state."

"Back exit through the footstools. Trolleyloads come up every day. Through the hall of the mother-vessels."

"What about all those . . . others?"

"Switch them off from the next hall."

"But the ones like you," Essa insisted.

"Brave all of a sudden, aren't you? Just get me out of here. That's your good deed for today."

Where was Soren? Soren the scrupulous. What would she think? Why wasn't she there to tell Essa what was right. Should she leave the hall full of wretched, twitching oldwomen, or end their mechanical existence with the dignity of human death? Was it cowardly to flee now with . . .

"I'm E'thane. Who are you?"

"Essa."

Why should she believe anything E'thane told her? Such a grisly story. It must be very depressing lying here day after day. Even the soundest mind would start to wander. And they did say that Tramontanes were inclined to emotion. Had she not herself been an Ack Ack, architected this edifice? Difficult to imagine those hard-working doctors were so unfeeling. Mustn't start getting squeamish about machinery. Very backward thinking. Essa collected herself. Know your limitations. When something is beyond you, you must tell those depending on you that they have asked too much.

E'thane reached for something in her pocket. Suddenly her arm was around Essa's neck, a sharp point pressed at Essa's throat.

"You get me the shit out of here, citizen, or I'll pump your veins full of air."

The Tramontane held a syringe to Essa's jugular.

"You can spend all your tomorrows on return trips."

There was nothing, E'thane found, like a syringe at the jugular to clear the synapses.

Essa worked methodically. Took a crepe bandage from the nurses' station, wound it round E'thane's arm.

"Loosen it for a few seconds every now and then. Don't want gangrene either. And before you start

85

cutting, make sure you got something to sew me up with."

Essa could find only a small blade and a reel of purple thread.

"Blade will have to do. But the thread's useless. Try that."

E'thane pointed to a length of catgut lying on the floor.

"It's not even sterile. You'll get blood poisoning."

"Later I'll get blood poisoning. Right now I want out. Run it under the tap."

Essa jabbed the curved blade of the knife into E'thane's wrist. She had to jerk it upward slightly, like a shovel clearing sewage. For second after second she hacked and hacked.

"You will say if it hurts?"

"It hurts."

Though she plunged the knife deeper and deeper into E'thane's arm, the metal seemed no nearer to the surface.

"Put your fingers in and pull."

"I feel sick."

"Here."

E'thane let go the syringe, placed Essa's hands either side of the wound.

"Hold it open. And look away."

E'thane stuffed her thumb and forefinger into the bubbling hole, located hard steel, and tugged. The tube came away in her hand with such a wave of blood both women were splattered. She stanched the flow with her palm.

"Sew me up."

Essa sewed carefully. It was hard to work the needle through human flesh. Often the wound was washed out by blood so that she could not see her stitches. Somehow it was over. E'thane was grey. The two oldwomen stared at E'thane's butchered arm, swollen as a corpse in water, red as liver.

"You take over," E'thane said.

Any minute the stitches would burst. All the blood

in E'thane's body would pour onto the floor. E'thane would faint from pain and Essa could not lift her. The nurses, tiring of Patient Y, would go strolling. Quietly as her beating heart allowed, Essa removed trays, cotton wool, swabs, dressings, bottles, graphs, spare towels from the nurses' station. She slid the shelves out of their sockets, wheeled the empty hull over to the bed, wedged E'thane between the back of the station and the handrail. Steadying herself on the rail, Essa began to trundle the contraption out under Abnormalidad Arch.

"Not that way," E'thane moaned, "Don't you think I'd have walked free years ago?"

Essa turned. Pushed the station down the hall toward the L bend. With each step the stench grew stronger.

An oldwoman hobbles, shuffles two paces, pauses, leans and catches breath. She pushes another old-woman, slumped, semi-conscious, feet dragging against the ground. Shrieks ring out suddenly and die away: "help me help me help me help me"; moans; restless sleep; a wracking cough followed by a high pitch whoop. A struggle for breath so regular it could pace the heart.

The rungs of the nurses' station tower above Essa's head. She cannot see where she is pushing. At the L bend she pauses. E'thane's out cold. From the right come the nurses' voices. To the left a narrow corridor slopes downward. Essa wheels to the left, though the corridor is dark, because she is tired and the slope will ease the weight. Miscalculation. The slope wrenches the station from Essa's hands, flings it helter skelter down the corridor into the darkness. Essa stumbles slowly after. The nurses hear a noise, but Patient Y picks the same moment to start up her scream. It has the urgent whine of a boiling kettle, the nurses rush to quell it. The station bumps against a buffer of laundry bags and comes to a standstill.

A cavernful of youngwomen lie in a dark red glow. The walls and the floor ripple slightly, as though filled tight with water. The heat is steady and intense. Into each woman's swollen abdomen is set a glass window allowing father-possessors to visit their prospective progeny. On the other side of the screen tiny sea horses float inside sealed bubbles. Essa fancies she can make out a hand, a foot, a human eye. She surveys the vessels which carry them. Some consist only of the abdomen and a valve to allow the seahorse to depart once optimum growth and full humanity have been achieved. The outer folds of the valve have been padded with hair. Many father-possessors caress it in their excitement at seeing their young take shape. Some like to make the initial deposit this way too. Where heads are lacking on individual abdomens, they have been tactfully replaced by a green metal box.

As she pushed E'thane's unconscious body down the hall of the mother-vessels, the rippling red light of the cavern upon them, Essa felt a certain tenderness for the one woman she was able to rescue. Long moments at a time, Essa was unaware whether she was saving E'thane's life, or E'thane hers. E'thane's will it was which propelled and guided them past the monstrous bellies, through the open doors of a lift. At the press of a button, instead of the cage moving up or down, the back wall split in two, revealing itself a goods exit. E'thane's will got them onto a conveyor belt disappearing into the fabric of the building. E'thane's will, too, which paused in the task of manoeuvring them both onto the belt, so near at last to safety, and insisted that Essa go back to the switch-board and turn off the life simulators. This time Essa heard E'thane's voice clearly, though the Tramontane's mouth and face were frozen.

"Those meters we passed. To the left of the exit arch. Remove the cover panel and reverse the dials. They'll die within two minutes of their next treatment."

Essa's body was not made for speed. Careful deliberation and an hour's early morning planning carried her gracefully through the day's obstacles. She cursed her slow, heavy legs which would not run lightly back through the lift cage to the switchboard. It took her so long to limp across from the goods exit that she feared someone would call the lift before she got through and she would be whisked off to some other part of the building, leaving E'thane on the conveyor belt. How would she find her way back? As she turned each dial round she thought of the oldwomen, their vital organs chained to electronic devices, the youngwomen, permanently pregnant. She, Essa, was deciding what life meant and what it did not mean. She had no recourse to city ordinances. It would have been a great relief to hear the Ideo Logician say that what she did was right.

Seventeenth Sighting: DEAD HEAT

The city missed its Ideo Logician. Without logic the ordinances were as tyrannical as the laws they replaced; the comforting filter was gone. No longer cheap help, the Tramontanes were cheap parasites with their great, brutish faces, too big for the city, slumped and stupid on the dust carts which no one saw them fill, leaning on municipal brooms which no one saw them sweep. Oboes were not fat and jolly but fat and wasteful, ought to be sliced down the middle, ate enough to feed two citizens. The new worry, that ageing was not as tidily cured by death as in previous decades, was spreading down from Ackademick zones, more prone to fancy and conjecture, to the concrete-thinking open market. The creeping fear, which could only ever be staved by frequent sex and heavy justification, the fear that women are incompatible with men's survival, a fear which required endless and increasing mollification, was turning to panic. Womb surrender was a marvellous innovation but needed the daily reinforcement of statistics and glad tidings to keep the fear at bay. When it comes down to it, youngwomen are different from youngmen.

If only the Ideo had prioritised raising male ratios, a vision of a future end to present inequality. Or justified the low rating, offered some new insight whereby the most obvious was not the best solution. Citizens were putting facts together for themselves. Logic failing, they turned to statistics and precedent. More nellies were hatched than zappers; more old-women sighted than oldmen; more youngwomen flaunted obesity; more female Trams in service than males. All those quiet, yielding bodies were conspiring to deprive, their passivity insurrection.

The citizens could not live without sense; they must make their own. As the absence of official explanation became more marked by increased duration, they found themselves forced to look about them, take note of surroundings they had scarcely glimpsed while the Ideo stood solicitous guard. Their specialities requiring exclusive concentration, they had hitherto entrusted their personal philosophy to common sense. But why should a subspecies be permitted through the city walls? How could a lower lifeform assimilate? In the first wave of logic-lost confusion Tramontanes were the clearest target. Dependent for their truth and efficacy on frequent repetition, the old saws: "Zurban backs free citizen brains"; "Open city – hopeful city", were soon discarded. The open market took logic into its own, inexperienced hands. One night five Tramontane compounds were set on fire. No one knew exactly how many were burned to death as no one knew for certain how many lived there, it being difficult to tell one Tram from another.

The Ackademick zone was swift to protest the "sheer barbarity; no way to treat guest workers and innocent servants". For was not this carnage really a blow at themselves? Few open market fathers could afford paid nursemaids, for all the wombs their women surrendered. Jealousy was ever a powerful motivator to the simple-minded.

A nightly exodus of Tramontanes crept over the walls into the Scrub to wait out the new violence. As the citizens began to shed their carefully acquired ignorance, they had to notice that the streets were dirtier, the piles of rubbish higher. Before, if they woke early, they could look out, watch the gutters hosed and the skips changed, the full ones winched up onto the transporter on clanking chains; bear silent witness to the glimmering streets, sluiced with water and shining like polished stone, a clean slate on which to inscribe a new day. Now the skips stood unemptied; yesterday's leavings were still there tomorrow.

There was, at first, a citizenly pride in the volume of consumption indicated; a vigorous capacity to leave ones mark; a certain asymmetric beauty in the brightly coloured wrappers flapping in a landscape of right angles and glass. No privacy of memories; the impartial wind opened clumsy wrappings, laying out burnt breakfast, torn love letters, bloody rags to the next passerby. Garbage sacks lined the kerb, leaking into the road. Drivers swerved constantly to avoid toppling litter, and a small landslide blocked the junction slipway to the northbound conduit.

Only the Acks were steadfast in their admiration. It required height and distance to regard those ever-growing piles, seething and swaying under some infestation of their own, with liberal enthusiasm. The open-market, by nature less philosophical, moved by self-interest where the Acks were securely tenured out of reach of contingency, were impatient with the rubbish and vicious to the few Tramontanes still within the precincts. The city hoses coiled neatly round the city hydrants, the skip transporters sparkled in orderly rows at the recycle plant. Soon there would be shortages in an already straitened environment. Without the daily tonnage of used commodities, no more could be reprocessed. The stockpiles dwindled rapidly; the city began to eat its sealed reserves, slow suicide while there was no way of replenishing.

Still no citizen lifted a finger. The principles of specialisation decreed that whoever first bent to remove leschugam from the heel of his boot and, instead of dropping it onto the pavement, placed it out of the way of fellow citizens, was then more fitted to

93

repeat the action. One Ack, absorbed in the administrative problems caused by the current emergency, turned from the spectacle of rubbish piling at his walls and asked what lesson was to be learned. Slogans, while adequately backing continuity, could not cope with introducing social change. With the sudden leap of genius, he forged the connection no one expected, the connection which, once made, no one can imagine the world without.

"The role of Tramontanes must be replanned. We need them to trade and work the plant outside the walls, but if our rubbish is recycled by them, our young cleaned and fed by them, we make ourselves vulnerable to their absence. We cannot trade with servants and we have a class of servants of our own, though they mutilate their bodies to prove this isn't so. Equalops and womb surrender have been a gallant effort but who is changing nappies now with the Tramontane nursemaids away? The elder sisters, of course. Who is picking over garbage in the street with a sharp eye for things of use? The youngwomen. We do not need to descend to the citlet compound to see the nappies changed, set up spyholes in the street to watch the gleaners. In a word: why use Tramontanes where female citizens will do?"

His scientific colleagues applauded.

"It puzzled us that high male sex ratios were rejected without justification. We hypothesized a ski injury to the Ideo Logician. But consider: the open market finds it hard to follow abstracts whereas rotting garbage is difficult to forget. Untutored, they see a surplus of women, feel instinctively that more men are the answer. The Ideo reminds them we are a city built on autonomy, we cannot allow our servants to become indispensable nor should the open market educate their daughters into incapacity for hard work. We do not want gender parity but an elite of zappers and a swarm of nellies. Saving your honour."

The honour in question was that of a female Ack

who, as long as her honour was saved, saw only benefit in her greater scarcity. Womb surrender showed wonderful dedication in those who were bred to it, but the indiscriminate spread of the practice amongst those who merely wanted status and freedom from plumbing threatened to reduce all post-operatives to faddish flutter-byes.

Thus was it argued in the Ackademick zone. The open market dealt differently with changes. Adjusting as they could to life where the day's dirt was not tidied away at dawn, they recovered a sense of history, of cause and effect, even of personal responsibility. Many were the highs of that first feeling of individual importance, that unless you did it, it would not get done and, if you did it, it would remain done next day. Many were the acts of misguided bravery as inexperienced minds set to righting civic injustice. They ranged from the grandiose and impersonal to the small but intimate. From the sickies in the Après-Ski Tower whose oxygen was thinned to lessen the burden on the city, to the forty year old women with dyed hair, shaved to brand them rejuvenators, to the small Tramontane buying linctus for a hacking cough told to 'sign here' and 'read the instructions' once it became clear he was illiterate.

Exit from the rubbish impasse was perceived by many persons concurrently though attributed to the most highly placed individual. An Ack rolled up his sleeves.

"Come on," he said from his tower window, "We must be flexible. Let's get to work; this is a municipal crisis."

Once the crisis was declared the citizens all mucked in together: Acks and open market, zapper and nelly, father and citlet alike. The streets were cleared in a matter of hours, shoulder rubbed against shoulder, not only was it a damned fine city, but they were damn fine chaps, every great or lowly one of them. The brotherhood of the battle line.

Down the street walked an oboe. She trod carefully, if massively, her steps smooth, avoiding any extra swing of flesh, thighs apart, braced like a rider's, arms graceful at her sides resisting each urge to tug the suit top down over her waist, that ineffectual twitch which marks the vulnerable, the ones who want the ground to swallow them up. Her breath was even, studied. She wore formal costume. Though jiggle suits were welcoming in their easy give and take, the elastic contours moulded themselves on the body so that every ripple of fat was starkly outlined. Costume is constricting, but it lends shape and anonymity to its wearer.

The pavement narrowed where a shopfront projected. The two youngmen behind the oboe would find it difficult to overtake her without breaking step with each other. The oboe, anticipating this impasse, speeded up. This only confirmed her predicament. Had she slowed, the youngmen might have passed her before the straits, but it is never safe for a fat woman to dawdle and the oboe was flustered. A blind friend was following, ten paces back, and, as she was also fat, it was naturally impossible for the two to walk together, even where the pavement permitted. Would the blind woman be confused by the sound of the youngmen's footsteps?

"Like overtaking a whale," observed one youngman.

"Or a monster slug," refined his friend.

"Stuffed slug in that costume."

"Would you like to lose weight? Ask me how."

"Well, slug, ask him."

"How?" asked the oboe.

"Try a full sentence."

"How do I lose weight?"

"Cut you down to half the size."

"Trim away unwanted fat."

"Display those fine bones you got under . . . What the shit . . . ?"

****

96

"The flayed torso of a man has been found in a plastic bag in the burn-out park. A left leg, left hand and right foot had been deposited in smaller bags in the vicinity. Citizens' watch state that none of the limbs belong to the same body. Though all are male."

"Get carried away?" said Desde when the report came over the speakers.

"We stabbed two hearts," said Soren, "the rest they did to each other."

"With holes in their hearts?"

"Not them. Other youngmen."

"Turn that thing off," yelled a voice from the dance floor. "This is a party."

"Switch out the voice but leave the seefax," advised Malachi, "so we can see if anything happens."

"If you happen to be looking at the screen when it does," said Soren.

"Alright, keep the sound low so only Soren can hear. She does boast how her hearing's not directional."

"Nor optional. Why should I be on duty all night?"

They turned the screen down to newsflash, timed for ten minute intervals.

"Did you really kill those youngmen?" The question sounded naive enough to warrant answering and the answer would echo and re-echo as each party guest arrived and heard the news. Gossip might as well relay the explanation while it mulled over the event. Though Soren was impatient of naivety. An ungenerous impatience and she disliked herself for it. Surely it was good to believe in a city where strangers on street corners are not feared but asked directions, offered help. But what fatal irresponsibility to behave as though that safe city were here.

"We have to kill," replied Soren, carefully.

"That reduces us to their level," the inevitable comeback.

"Yes," Soren agreed, "They have accomplished that. Except that we can only kill. We cannot warn or wound, we have no symbol of power with which to make a threat."

The room absorbed her response and argued it out in corners. Soren wanted a respite from bravery in which to mourn the dead. The physical details, the urgent intimacy which bound the killer to the killed, the dread beforehand that she would not be strong enough, skilled as she was, were already stamped on her mind. The elements of future nightmares chiselled themselves off from the mass of impressions and filtered down to add another sediment to the bedrock of fear.

"Bound, you and I, now," Malachi was saying.

"But not frozen," Soren returned, "We can make of it what we want."

It was not conversation Soren wanted now but Essa. Essa, warm, naked and miraculous. Essa's skin was always miraculous when Soren first touched it again. It made Soren feel real, entire, up against the very boundaries of herself along the line that closed her in and joined her to the world. The line of Essa's skin on hers.

"We killed two people," she would tell Essa.

Not, "We killed two youngmen," as she must say, correctly, to the questioning Senectity. Essa would accept 'people'. That was the way she thought. Soren could groan,

"How many of us must kill before this is over?"

Essa would not add reprovingly,

"How many more be killed?"

So often at these gatherings Soren, Malachi, Karlin and Desde sat by the back wall, hogging the radiant, throwing politics back and forth, while the others danced and Essa hovered. Essa would interrupt with enthusiasm and throw down her views on the subject under discussion. They would wait politely till she had finished, pick up the lost thread and continue. At first Soren would excuse herself and invite Essa to dance, though it was well known that it terrified her to enter the circling throng. Everyone would be careful, but Soren could feel their heroic effort not to brush against her and it irked to place herself so entirely in their protection. Essa, of course, refused. Soren trembling and miserable was not the woman she had fallen in love with. So Essa flirted with Desde and when they danced discussion faltered, for Essa well-partnered was exquisite. Then the table thought it glimpsed what Soren might admire in her. Essa's pavanne was graceful and stately, her sense of rhythm precise, almost imperious. It spoke of discipline, of order, raised above brute convention to a spirit of warmth, generosity, a holding up, not a holding back.

Soren found comfort in missing Essa, longing for her humanism, her indiscriminate compassion.

"It was us or them," pursued Malachi, "And either way we'd lose."

"Yes," Soren agreed, "but we can minimise the loss."

"The way those bodies were cut up, no one will imagine two fat oldwomen stabbed their hearts."

"I'm not concerned with citizens' watch."

"You should be. At any moment . . . "

"You're right," Soren sighed, "At any moment, yes, any moment. And I am concerned. I'm a concerned citizen. I don't want to live in a city where oldwomen are despised, where fat is shredded, where the pride of youth skin each other's corpses. But I know about that, I'm part of a movement for change. What I don't know is who is coming with me."

"Or where we're going," finished Malachi.

"So many of the Senectity act like killing is sin."

"They don't want to become people who have killed."

"They want to keep their ideal of a good city by acting like it's here already. Only young Ackademicks can do that, because they don't really live in it."

"Perpetually passing through."

"And occasionally glancing out the window."

"So where is Essa tonight?" asked Desde, sitting down with them in the radiant corner.

"I've no idea," snapped Soren, "We were talking about the Senectity."

"You and Essa had a row?"

"As it happens. I'll get a pot of akyan. Could do with some ingestible comfort."

Soren stood up, felt for her cane and began to tap her way to the food hatch. She moved slowly, steadily, so the others would see and get out of her way. Scarcely three steps later someone patted her hand and asked if she wanted help. Soren smiled graciously.

"I was going to fetch akyan."

"You sit down. I'll get it for you."

"We're fussy, I'm afraid," Soren smiled again, "We like it hot and strong, the water fresh, oxygenated and boiling."

"I know what you mean," the other woman sympathised, "I'll bring a selection."

"And if there were any jumpcakes . . . "

"Works every time," Malachi mouthed to Desde.

"It's because she's blind," Desde shrugged.

"It's because she's Soren," Malachi corrected, "Look at all the other blind women lucky to get a place in the queue, let alone told when it's their turn."

"Soren does push it with the pathetic blind number," Desde continued.

"Nothing pathetic about her, only very desirous and very grateful," Malachi retorted, "You don't object when she appropriates the warmest corner of the room."

"And gets them to turn down the bass," Desde agreed.

Soren sat down again. Malachi poured.

"They feel uncomfortable to be caught out in a compromise," said Malachi, pursuing the earlier theme, "That's why they're giving us a hard time."

"We all compromise," said Soren, "between the ideal and the street. But there's no safety in pretending the street's negotiable. When someone's offering to slash you, you have to get them first."

"How do you know you'll manage it?" threw in Desde.

"You only know you have to," said Soren.

"Skill, constant practice and a sharp knife help," added Malachi.

"But you're neither of you strong," Desde objected.

Soren's impatience rose. The mechanics were not new to Desde, why was she too treating the killers as curiosities? How many of the Senectity had already killed? Soren pulled her knife from her sleeve.

"Here," she exclaimed, waving it at Desde. "It's springloaded and sonar equipped – tuned to the heartbeat. All you need is a steady hand."

She pressed the trigger and the thin steel blade shot out like a lazer, two feet from the knife.

"It's best to get them from the back," she went on, "Oldwomen can't afford heroics."

Above the noise of the music and the dancing, women's voices calling greetings, came a single, flawless soprano:

"Here I stand with my knife in my hand."

An alto joined it, then a mezzo in perfect, abrupt harmony, the last note lying jagged on the air as the mezzo finished the round.

"I can't handle this," said Malachi.

"Let them sing," said Soren, "It's a hard life."

Those who called the Senectity extremist, not knowing what its outer limits were, fearing it had none, rallied beneath the sarcastic refrain. There was Soren, leader of the leaderless, who had personally collected many of the oldwomen now assembled. There was the knife clasped tight in her hand. What would she stop at? Sides were a while forming, misgivings great. This was the oldwoman who had left food on the doorstep, in the alleyway, the hidey-hole, night after night until the receiver, compelled by hope, exhaustion, curiosity, came out of her lair to glimpse her benefactor's face. Or to sniff out traps. Sometimes, on seeing another oldwoman, her short-lived hope would drain away; she would hurry Soren inside, protesting that she had enough to worry her without adding to the burden by looking out for

101

someone else. Then Soren could set to work. Sometimes the regular gifts were too much. Soren would only know of her failure when the food was left untouched; then she might smell the rank odour of a corpse, or be forced to conclude that the oldwoman had fled to another hole where no-one spied on her. But the rest, and there were a hundred successes to each despair, were slowly enticed out of hiding, told of the existence of many more like themselves, offered safe refuge in the footstools of the Ackademy until they found accommodation elsewhere.

It was said, also, that Soren would explain the bonds of the Senectity were strong because the oldwomen loved each other, and to disbelievers she would demonstrate. This was as true as it was untrue, Soren said. It depended how she felt about the woman in question and she did not need disbelief to spur her on. The same, she added, could be said of any relationship. Nor was Soren the only member of the Senectity who sought to dig out oldwomen from the wreckage, but she was the one who was remembered, and such was her personal renown that even those who were exhumed by other hands would boast that it was Soren sought them out.

While the sides gathered, Soren was listening intently. Above their heads, somewhere in the shafts and conduits of the building, she could hear a rushing sound, like water. A burst pipe? But the noise was moving fast: something sliding down a tunnel. Soren tuned out the hall and concentrated. A sudden loud bump. A bang.

"Citizens' watch," yelled an accusing voice. "They followed you here after the murders."

"They'll get us. All in one go."

"We're trapped."

"Nonsense," said Malachi quickly, getting to her feet and turning the picture on, "It's probably the screen; we tuned it to newsflash and it's about time for another one."

Soren walked toward the side door.

"Where's she going?"

"Don't let her out."

"Something's fallen down the laundry chute, that's all," said Soren calmly, "Who's coming with me to check it out?"

Desde was first to reach the mouth of the chute. Lying on the conveyor belt were the bodies of two oldwomen.

"Revenge," she muttered, "So we have been found out."

"Don't be ridiculous," snapped Soren, "A tooth for a tooth is for those in equality. We are not on those terms with the city."

The bodies were warm. One groaned. With great strain the top woman was rolled off the other. It was Essa. The news sent fresh fears rippling through the crowd: had the Après-Ski Tower heard the commotion? But, once it was learned that the women were alive, there was a bustle of stretchers, trolleys and bandages purposeful enough to blunt the edge of acrimony. Still quarrelling nervously, groups of party guests gathered to disperse: one oldwoman every five minutes. Though it was the early hours of the morning, and the streets were empty, it did not do to flaunt in rowdy bevies.

Soren slept that night beside Essa. Things were as bad as they could be without snapping. The city was closing in, the Senectity so scared they were fleeing their own shadow. Euphoria at the sheer numbers of oldwomen unearthed was giving way to dread that their great number would wipe them out. Essa had been in an accident and she, Soren, had killed. But despite these obvious ills, Soren felt easier than she had for a long time, and for a long time, as she lay awake, listening for Essa's breathing, she could not think why. She was happy, joyous; something good had happened. At last she remembered. Karlin. Karlin had said she was getting better.

Eighteenth Sighting: THE ECSTATIC
PRESENT

Interim Two was bleak and windswept, a narrow ledge between mountain and ocean, sheer rock looming behind, sheer cliff dropping away in front. No way out, or in, save along the aerial cable which carried the hanging gazibus. Passengers stared vainly at the mountain wall, dizzily down the cliff-face, a careful foot from the edge, then huddled disconsolate on the bench and studied the timetable. Though some, bored or cold, had tried to scale the mountain, few even looked to the cliff: a cursory glance showed how it bulged like a forehead, then swung back in a hollow, a fifty foot drop to the next horizontal. Plenty more prestigious climbs higher up if you were going to mess with ropes.

Certainty and desperation worked where idle curiosity waned. Scimitel headed straight for the cliff, walked out along the forehead, then, scared the wind would blow her over, sat down and edged forward till her legs dangled in empty air. Beneath her feet was a narrow rocky tongue leading in toward the hollow. She gave it a tentative kick; a slither broke off and skipped down the cliff. She had shifted too much weight forward to retreat and found herself slipping with nothing but smooth rock to cling to. The tongue would have to hold. Like a tightrope walker she trod along the ribbon of rock as it followed the curve of the hollow. Concentrating on placing one foot exactly in front of the other, aware of every twitch of muscle, she failed to notice when she touched the floor of the cavern. Not yet daring to look down, she maintained her cautious progress, fearing some new obstacle. Expecting her path to continue its descent she dug her foot into the ground, lost her balance and, with terror, stumbled. The irregular running steps which right a stumble, propelled her into a rock wall. At last she looked around and found herself in the mouth of an enormous chasm leading into the mountain, seeming to lose itself in there, it was so dark and silent. She walked a determined two paces before her nerve failed and she crumpled behind a massive boulder, waiting to feel again more scared of the known than the unknown.

At first Scimitel assumed she had made her up. She had sat so long in the dark on that cold rock floor, shivering with retrospective fright, wishing she could see, wishing the tall stranger were there to protect her. After a while she had indeed been able to make out the shape of rocks and boulders in the grey light and, as she stared, testing out this new skill, suddenly she saw her, the enormous woman, the one who lifted cars.

Ithaca strode into the mouth of the tunnel wondering why no one knew of it, so close to the Interim. For a moment she stood still, getting used to the dark. But, as there was no more light ahead, she decided to go on, trusting to luck and muscle.

Scimitel got to her feet. She would run after the tall stranger, tell her she had left homesafe forever and would follow wherever she led. Then she saw the second one, outside on the rock ledge. The light confused and dazzled her. There were two of them? Two women like that?

Zay had followed Ithaca closely from the footstools of the Ackademy, only momentarily thrown by the sight of the silver Quantum parked on top of the detches. A moment's memory of her ex-lover's careless generosity told her the car had been offered in payment of the fortune teller's services. Ithaca would not leave town without a reading. Zay was a restless mixture of anger and misery; the sooner she ended it the better.

Scimitel waited, silent behind her boulder, the habit of hiding and long thought too strong to break on a momentary enthusiasm. She watched her saviour walk into the tunnel, in slow motion, as though she moved through water. Then, behind her, came the other one, (shorter and slighter now that close comparison was possible) her arms were outstretched, as though to hug an old friend, but in her hands she held a garrotte. Scimitel lost her fear of unconsidered action.

"Watch out," she shouted and her thin, piping voice bounced round the walls of the cavern.

The two women in the cave vanished; one with her arms still held out, the other turning back to see who was behind. They disappeared as swiftly as if the rock beneath their feet had crumbled and plummeted them into the ocean. Scimitel found herself venturing into the tunnel, her slow, faltering pace caused not by nerves, but the pressure of an air current blowing against her, pinning her to the wall. She struggled on, trusting more to insignificance and slight build than any strength of hers to fight the wind. The current was weaker along the wall, slowed by friction of irregular stone. Then, as suddenly as the women in front of her, Scimitel too was picked up and flung down the tunnel. Sometimes the wind dropped and she felt herself falling to the ground, only to be snatched up again by another gust.

There was light now, dim and green but enough to see the dimensions of the tunnel, the trailing vegetation through which they were passing: thick moss and fungus clinging to damp walls, the long twisted roots of trees. Ithaca was caught by a clump of knotted dodder. Zay, once more, was thrown against her, garrotte in hand. Scimitel, snared further back in the fronds of a creeper, was unable to reach her hero.

"Watch out," she shouted again, and again her voice echoed.

Once more Ithaca and Zay were freed, their frozen cameo smashed by the fierce wind, and again Scimitel came after them, near enough to watch, too far to intervene. Bounced from wall to wall, saved from broken bones by pockets of air which slowed her flight, Scimitel would pass within an inch of Ithaca's face, arched with surprise or Zay's, carved with hate.

Until with another, last turn in the tunnel, three bodies were spat out into sunlight. Each lay, a separate heap upon the ground, the wind knocked out of them. Behind towered green hills, rising crag upon crag into a sky so blue it went on forever. In front spread a flat sheet of water, smooth enough to reflect each shade of rock like a second valley. Scimitel opened her eyes and stared, so confused still from the whirling of the tunnel that she was unsure whether she'd been thrown onto her stomach, and was gazing at a reflection in water, or onto her back to feast on the sky.

Ithaca was first to stir. The light hurt her eyes as before the shade had clouded them. She looked back at the rock to see where they had come out, but could distinguish nothing in the green folds save some yellow and blue specks she took for sweet wrappers. She ought to mark this bank so they'd find it on the way back. She must get on.

Zay's body was so twisted her arms seemed to have corkscrewed round her body, face ground into the dirt, mouth full of earth. She ignored all but her sense of betrayal, guarded closely since her discovery at Ithaca's residence.

"I'm going to kill you," she hissed, partly to remind herself.

"No," said Scimitel, still gazing far up the mountain, or was it down into the water, "She saved my life."

"Who're you – the new cunt-licker? She saved

your life! She ruined mine – and all the other city Tramontanes'."

"Neither," Ithaca remarked easily, "Neither saviour nor destroyer."

"Don't tell me you were only doing your job," Zay sneered. The garrotte clenched between her fists, but she needed surprise to best Ithaca.

"I keep things quiet so they don't get worse," Ithaca offered, "I make each feel that all is as it ought and in his best interests."

"You keep them quiet so you keep power."

Scimitel was trying to pant, but each time she breathed she felt a knife at her ribs. Listening to the angry voices she wished she could move; it was all she could do to stare upwards and wait for the pain to stop. Even that strip of sky looked different: brighter, higher, bluer than in the city. The air was so clean she wanted to swallow it. She would leap to her hero's defence, if only she could leap, if only she could understand the argument. Sometimes you thought grown-ups were quarrelling and it turned out to be foreplay. The shorter one said, "cunt-licker". Scimitel stuck her tongue out and licked the air. "Cunt", she thought. Did women do that? She thought about the whispers and the nellies in her homesafe. They did it. She remembered. Or she'd always known. Scimitel listened again.

"I don't have power, only privilege," Ithaca objected, safe from physical attack while Zay was too exhausted to stand up. Zay's pride would never accept a beating and Ithaca needed her ex-lover to help find the Scrub-dwellers. "For myself, I'm a female Tram who likes older women. For the city I'm the Ideo, a youngman from the Ackademick Zone. I explain, I don't make it up."

"A Tram? So you're a Tramontane when it suits you too."

"You knew that," said Ithaca, "I toasted you. On the foreshore."

Zay remembered. They had made love on the beach

and she had been happy. At last, someone who knew what it was like to come from outside the city. But she'd been wrong.

"You don't know what it's like to be a woman, let alone a Tramontane," she shouted, feeling tears rise.

"I do know," Ithaca shouted back, "That's why I am the way I am. I got the choice between 'sir' and 'darling' and I picked 'sir'."

"You chose between tyrant and trampled," Zay retorted.

"Who do I tyrannise?"

"You named them: women, Trams, oboes, sickies, baskets . . . "

"My lover is an oldwoman," Ithaca flung back, "It was you used to say that sucking an old . . . "

"I saved her, your oldwoman, your precious Karlin."

"You did what to her?"

"She was keeling over. Someone would have done her. I escorted her to a car to see her home."

"Lies," said Ithaca with contempt, "Karlin's far too security-conscious. She'd never let a strange young-woman take her . . . "

"I didn't take her. I told you, I got her to a car. I mean, I called a car but she wouldn't get in it. I rescued her from the others, though. They would have killed her. Put her head under the hot tap; her wig and everything came away."

"Vicious thugs."

"But I got her out," Zay insisted.

"So you say."

"Yeah, while you were off playing the Ack. Not much of a man if you can't protect your woman."

Not much of a man to stand here arguing while Karlin failed. Not much of a man at all.

"Zay, Karlin's sick. I was sent here for the cure. Will you help?"

Zay had finally managed to roll over and stare at Ithaca's face. The sight of the woman she loved, lying beside her, after the longing, the fears, and the fury, moved her. In vain she told herself this was the woman who had left her, who betrayed her. The old feeling that Ithaca was always right took over; Ithaca would explain why she had broadcast those lies, how subtly seditious they were in fact. She was as wayward and as stubborn, as well-meaning, as opportunistic and as generous as she'd always been; Zay had missed her. Did Ithaca really believe that broad shoulders and iron muscles convinced anyone? If they looked even twice they could see she was a female who had never been made a woman let alone a man. But Ithaca was not asking Zay to have her back; she was asking her to help Karlin.

It seemed to Scimitel, lying on the ground, watching the clouds, that the two big women were still in the tunnel, able to see each other but no more. Despite the growing heat, the pool of sweat accumulating down her back, Scimitel was pleased with herself. The moss beneath her hands welcomed her. She patted it lazily; water squelched through her fingers, cool and fresh. She dabbed her cheeks and forehead. Long habit told her she must stay on guard, but she could sense no present danger and she longed to believe that fear was over. The moss was delicious, she sucked a lump thirstily, filling her dry mouth with a pleasant earthy taste.

"It's very hot," she said to the others, "And there's no protective filter out here."

Her body was almost hidden under zapper apparel, but her face was beginning to feel prickly. Whenever her hatch went skiing, it was always she who burned just looking at the sun. She surveyed her two companions: her hero was dark-skinned and shielded by her white ackademickal, but the other was light, the lurex one-ply torn in many places exposing her skin to whatever whirled in the atmosphere.

"You're burning," Scimitel said, tapping Zay on the shoulder.

Zay spun round.

"You'll feel it later," Scimitel continued.

"We'd better find a food station," said Ithaca.

111

"Isn't one," said Scimitel, "Not as far as I can see. No walkways either. More like the snowslopes."

"Only there's no snow," said Zay, who had never been skiing but knew not to admit it. She could skate better than anyone.

Ithaca turned two full circles: nothing she recognised, all curves, no identifiable straight lines or corners. Like a vast burn-out park without flower bed or ash mound. As the little one said, snow slopes without snow. Underfoot was soft and elastic, everywhere deep green merging to blue: sky, ground and all this herbaceous stuff in the middle. However did the Scrub-dwellers find their way around?

"They said it was like this," said Zay bitterly. She had always hoped she might find something to be proud of out here. "Nothing moves, nothing sounds and all you feel is the force of gravity."

"We can't just stay here waiting for direction," said Ithaca, "Have you and your friend decided whether you're coming with me? You might as well since you've followed me this far."

"I'll go with you," said Scimitel quickly.

Ithaca studied her. Such a small, pale thing, what made her think she was going anywhere? What induced Zay to bring her?

"Looks like your friend's decided for you," Ithaca turned to Zay.

"I'm Scimitel," the little one piped up, "Scimitel Ekkos, Open Market." No need to admit she was still a nelly. Besides, if the fortune-teller was right, she was being spoken for at this very moment.

Ithaca bowed. "Ithaca Benaccar, Status Six."

Scimitel knew it was an Ack grade, but you could see that from the gown. What she could never remember was how the numbers went. She smiled encouragingly and looked impressed. Her hero was much better close up, no one but a fool would think her a man. She was tall, broad and solid with a straight jaw and fierce eyes but her voice was high. And she looked angry, like someone who would have

112

to take care of you when you got tired, not indulgent like a father with a runaway nelly.

"Zay Liebling, Assimilate. Ithaca, what the pus did you bring the little one for? What's the point of fobbing her onto me? Got plans for the two of us?"

"No one brought me," Scimitel protested, "I ran away."

The others exchanged glances.

"I saw you," Scimitel continued to Ithaca, "You picked up that detch in your own two hands and you turned it around in the air. But I knew you were a woman. You came to me with a zapper suit."

"I didn't come to you," said Ithaca, "I've never laid eyes on you before. You dreamed it. Go on homesafe before your father misses you."

"Don't rub it in," said Zay, "You know what their fathers do to them."

"How?" Scimitel demanded, ignoring Zay's interruption. They all said it was a crying shame, meaning you to cry and feel ashamed.

In vain three pairs of eyes searched for the tunnel exit. They were surrounded by rocks a hundred different colours and all of them green.

"Go home any way you like," said Ithaca, "You can't come with us, it's too important."

"You don't even know where you're going," Scimitel challenged.

Ithaca took off her white ackademickal and wrapped it round Zay.

"Besides," Scimitel's eyes gleamed, "I can be useful to you."

"Yeah?" said Zay.

"It's too late covering her up in that cloak," Scimitel continued to Ithaca, "She's burnt now."

"It's better than nothing."

"I've got something to show you," said Scimitel.

She dropped to the ground, scooped up a lump of moss and held it out to Zay.

"Put this on your shoulders," she urged, "I rubbed some on my neck, it draws the sting out."

Zay shrugged, she was still clutching the garrotte. Scimitel stood on tiptoe and pressed the wet clod to Zay's upper arm, now so red it must blister. A sudden burning pain shot through at the touch, but it passed quickly leaving a soothing coolness.

"How did you know?" asked Zay, rewinding the garrotte and stuffing it inside the lurex so she could apply moss to any skin that had been exposed.

"I guessed. Or else it was a folktale my nursemaid told me."

"There's a lot of hidden benefits in the Tramontane nursemaid," Ithaca observed.

"Any gentleness the citizens possess they learned from their nursemaids," added Zay, "Every last one of them, reared by a Tram."

This Zay was so angry with the citizens, Scimitel was tempted to give herself away and announce that she was only a citlet.

"You can come with us," Ithaca was saying, "Until we find a way to send you back. But you'll have to keep up."

"You've decided I'm coming too," said Zay.

"Aren't you?"

"Where are you going?"

"Up into the mountains; I'll be able to see better where we are."

"No," said Scimitel decisively, "We should follow the water. My legs wouldn't get me up that mountain and if there are people here, they'll be living where the water is."

It made sense.

"Why did you say all that stuff, Ithaca? 'If zurbans wish to live in the city as Tramontanes, their unit hour must have the lowest possible value. In a city where time is rationed to maximise enjoyment, outsiders must be rationed doubly.'?"

"Tramontanes are outsiders," Ithaca insisted, "It's what the word means."

"It's you that decides what words will mean."

"Not on my own. They wouldn't work unless

everyone else recognised them too. Tramontanes come from Tramontana. They wear badges, for shit's sake, 'Out and Proud'. Go on about their rich cultural heritage. Well they can't have the best of both worlds."

"But why should they have the worst? Some of us have never set foot in Tramontana. We're as much part of the city as you are."

"As me? As me? Precisely. I'm a Tramontane. My mother was a Tramontane."

"It's almost impossible to tell."

"Good," Ithaca bellowed up the mountain. "I act the citizen, I get the benefits of the citizen. And so do you, Zay."

"Why aren't you claiming the benefits of Tramontana? Think about that."

"This green wilderness? You want to reclaim it?"

Scimitel had been trudging for ages behind Ithaca. At first she had skipped and hopped, feasted on the broad, lapping lake and the blue immensity of the mountains. Now she was too tired to pay attention to anything but the prints of Ithaca's boots in which she placed her own, every third step. If they made progress, she was unable to discern it. One bit of lake looked so much like another, and the rocks seemed to follow them down the valley. She longed for a rest she dared not ask for. They were rushing headlong for nowhere.

"Zay, the anguished questions would sound a lot more convincing if I couldn't hear 'And why did you leave me?' whining at the back of every one of them."

"That's low," said Zay, "I must have really got to you. You know your job consists of making the murderers comfortable and the victims responsible. That little nelly . . . "

"She's called Scimitel."

"You remembered her name. Did you notice the scars on her ankles when she took her boots off? I've seen them in the citlet compounds practising walking with ropes between their legs. Was that necessary, Ithaca?"

"Fathers do that. I thought with equalops and womb surrender they'd calm down and rear the nellies like the zappers. Because there wouldn't be any difference."

"If there isn't any difference why do you prefer oldwomen?"

"Let's stop and rest," panted Scimitel. She didn't want to be implicated in their row if it was going to get nasty. It isn't safe to let tall women pick you up. They throw you in the air because they're happy, but if they get to see the mournful side of things they're quite likely to slouch off and leave you fall to the ground.

"Poor little dot. We should have slowed down."

"Compassion? What about your anti-weakness ordinances?"

"They are not mine. Your stupidity is dangerous."

"Sounds to me like I'm zeroing in."

"I accorded priorities. I justified. Common sense passed them. The citizens are not empty vessels to have opinions poured smoothly down their throats. When my father, Benaccar, Status Six, had run out of cynicism and was casting about for a new Ideo Logician, I suggested interim measures to keep the more aggressive elements at bay. I reckoned it would take a great burden off the Ideo if the citizens could be persuaded to provide raw material themselves, and outrage is the most effective short-term opinion-maker going. It wipes history from your head and fills you with horror of the present evil, purified of wider context which might moderate reaction. The biggest problem to justify to everyone's satisfaction is always the differences between men and women. This was before they had equalisation to look forward to. I invited youngwomen from all walks of life: Ack, Tram, Open Market, Assimilatory; fit or obese; nelly or spoken-for, to write their own stories, sparing no detail. Youngwomen reading these stories felt that their truth was, at last, being told. Now the world would hear how badly treated, overworked, under-

116

paid and unappreciated they were, how awful were their lives. It was possible for those who wrote the stories to become rich on the proceeds. Women came to believe this was possible on a wider scale. Youngmen, on the other hand, read the stories and were pleased that youngwomen were indeed being kept underfoot, reassured that nothing had changed since the last book. It was quite a task to discover new areas of female exploitation to expose for the civic fix."

"Manipulation."

"Another word for lying, but those women write straight from the heart. If I told them that men enjoy female-victims, they would agree with me and they wouldn't see what it had to do with them. If I told them to ease up and suggest a little light, they would tell me they were not prepared to let men off the hook."

"What about women?"

"They felt, and I agreed, that it was inappropriate to describe the sort of comfort and joy women give each other in books to be read in the open market. They thought men would enjoy it salaciously; I thought men would burn it as sedition. The effect was the same: no one wrote of it."

Scimitel leaned her cheek against a rough, lichen-covered rock, and gave in to self-pity. A thin white puddle with blue veins. Not even thinness she could be proud of, but a harbinger of adipose surfeit.

"Moss is delicate. Tread once, it springs back. Tread a second time, it yellows, dries out, dies."

"As long as they don't retrace their steps."

"Why wait passively, fingers crossed?"

"So they plod back to their ' forsaken city and tell the world there's nothing here. All we need is travellers' tales."

"What if they're from the Senectity?"

Another nursemaid's tale: little people who lived inside the mountain and came out to dance at full moon. If once you hear them singing, beware. Only those

117

destined to join them are allowed to eavesdrop their deliberations. Scimitel smiled wryly to herself, if you stared long enough at the rocks you did start to imagine faces on them: huge, hooked noses, cavernous eyes, wrinkled skin hanging in dewlaps over scraggy necks. Scimitel tried to be sensible. There were large brown mushrooms growing between the rocks, and the moss here, sheltered in a hollow, was sprouting tender white shoots. She was hungry. She picked a mushroom and examined its silky skin, stroked its smooth head against her cheek. People died eating poisonous mushroom, but they also died of hunger. Someone had to test it out, and how could anything which felt so good betray you? All the same, she gathered a handful of moss sprouts first and crammed them in her mouth. She'd already eaten some moss, and that hadn't hurt her.

"There you are," said Ithaca, her enormous shadow darkening the hollow. So much more light and dark out here without the city filter. "I've found her."

Zay ran over, caught sight of Scimitel comfortably settled among the rocks, the curly shoots dangling from her mouth.

"Munching cress already. She's a fast learner."

Both the big women laughed at that. They laughed and laughed. Every now and then they pulled themselves together, drew breath and tried to speak, but they would meet each other's eyes and spark off again.

"What's so funny about eating cress? It tastes good."

"We know, we know," said Ithaca quickly. "You just look funny. I think we're both so tired and hungry we'd laugh at anything."

It wasn't fair of them to finish their row by laughing at her. If they'd been nellies from her homesafe, Scimitel would have had a lot to say about it.

"Ithaca," Zay snapped, getting angry again, "If she's coming with us, she has to understand our jokes. Cress is thick and curly, right? Like pubic hair."

"I see," said Scimitel gravely.

She didn't have any hair yet, but it would be a useful expression once she did. Eating pussy, sucking cunt, grazing, pearl diving, paying lipservice, going down on, performing cunnilingus, practising oral sex; Scimitel carefully added 'munching cress'. Oral sex. That had got a lot of laughs. In the twelfthday test at their homesafe, a sister nelly had punched out that oral sex meant 'talking about it'. The educator had surely passed this masterpiece of innocence to their father as the nelly was spoken for shortly after and disappeared from the compound. The world outside the citlet residence was full of silky mushrooms which might kill you, and words which turned out quite different than you thought.

Ithaca joined Scimitel in the rocky semi-circle, picked herself a handful of moss shoots, then started on the mushrooms. Scimitel watched. Nothing terrible happened so she chewed a piece of the mushroom in her hand. It was fleshy and tasteless.

"I don't understand this place," said Ithaca, "So pleasant, all blue and green, lush meadowland, bright sunlight but so quiet it deafens you. All you hear is silence. When you look at anything, try to pick out particulars, it melts back into everything else."

"This moss," added Zay, "Soft and springy, easy on the legs, but it's like walking on carpet. After a while you long for steel skates and rough concrete. We're sinking into the stuff, getting nowhere."

"I don't know where to look or what I'm looking for," Ithaca complained, "I'd move mountains for Karlin, fight a gallery of overjoying dopeheads, but there's no one here."

"In the city there's always someone. Something. Gulls overhead, flies buzzing round the bins, maggots seething on flesh. Not this nothing," said Zay.

"You start forgetting why you've come. Why it matters. You feel hungry, you eat a mushroom; you get tired, you sit on a rock. Simple. In the city you have to do things, prepare for things, recover from things, remember, rush."

119

"Do you think it's the mushrooms?" asked Scimitel anxiously.

"No. It's been like this since we arrived, seeping in. As though we're walking in snow, chilled to the marrow and we can't tell if we're burning from heat or cold," said Ithaca.

"Then you feel sleepy, you lie down in the soft snow for a rest, and seven days later your body's found by mountain rescue frozen solid."

"We've been here so long," said Zay, "And the sun hasn't set. Just gone on bright daylight. Ithaca's shadow's been short as a moss stalk and as long as a rock and still the sun hasn't gone down."

"Have you noticed the rocks?" asked Scimitel.

"Can't avoid them."

"They always seem to be the same ones, as though they were following us. Escorting us out of the valley."

"I don't like this place," said Zay vehemently. "I can't hear. I can't see. I don't understand anything and someone's smiling quietly, waiting for us to leave."

"The static present," murmured Ithaca.

"Ecstatic," Zay corrected.

"I introduced it as 'static' but the city found that pessimistic, unyouthful." Scimitel rummaged through her list of tenses. 'Ecstatic present – alternative term for present continuous.'

"The great soft warm golden treacle verb," Ithaca continued, laughing wryly. "Women writing life stories . . . "

Scimitel nodded. "We had to read them for home-work. Rub our noses in squalor. 'See how good your father is, saves you from such a life. If you ran away, look where you'd sink.' "

"Some of the authoresses were uneasy. Didn't think the message was getting through. Said the problem was process. Couldn't change the world without changing the way things were done. Said men tyrannise with nouns: great marble chunks of substantives with thick lines drawn round them. Said men go about naming things, creating hierarchies, setting things apart from each other solely because each bears a different name. Said women beware solid states, they work against you. We should distinguish only in terms of action, mindful that it all comes together at the endings; emphasise connectings. That's what I call the static present: verbs only, happenings not facts. No agents and no responsibility."

"But a verb, used as a noun, becomes a noun," quoted Scimitel.

"They got excited when they learned that Tramontanes only have verb forms. No rain, no snow, no love, no death. Instead it is raining, it is snowing, it is loving, it is dying. As though the molecules of this bit of world were at present forming love, but soon they'd move off and form something else: a jug, maybe, or a thousand acapella hosannas. The women called it process. It was bad translation. You can't speak Tramontane in a city without an '."

"But out here," said Zay, "we cannot distinguish. And it does hill, and it valleys and it mosses and it mountains and there is no agent. Look around: there is an it here."

"If you're going to get mystical, use the proper terminology," mocked Ithaca. "There is a being here and this being is greening."

"Ithaca," said Zay with uncharacteristic earnest, "That's what ' stands for: 'ing'. What's missing from the city. The longer you mock, the less chance we have of finding the words for this new thought."

"Different lifestyles use different constructions," said Ithaca evasively, "Running, jumping and leaping are not exactly unheard of."

Zay was stung. Whatever possessed her, Assimilate that she was, to defend the Scrub? Of course they used the present continuous in the city. It was no secret.

The three youngwomen were surrounded by rock. The hooked noses, cavernous eyes and wrinkled skin were more prominent since Scimitel had grown used to looking at them.

"Can you see us now? Since that sounds like your favourite sense." As before, the voice came from inside the rock.

Nineteenth Sighting: TWIN MAGGOTS

Pain in her head and stomach. Eyes burning, melting into her sockets. Die die death. Guts leaking out of her. Hours, days, twelfths, hours Scimitel lay in a dark place and someone came and put a rough wet towel on her forehead, then went away again. After a while the towel became a hand, the hand of a very old woman, a heavy, wrinkled hand and kind. The thing that used to be Scimitel was turning into a mass of ulcers, only the hand kept turning it back into a human being. The hand liked Scimitel, it soothed, and cooled the fires, drew the pain into a corner so she could feel other things again.

An enormous cavern full of water, so dark you could not see, but the echoes bounced a measured pace. You could tell the ceiling was high, the walls wide by listening to the sounds rebound. Very little was lost of heat or noise via the entranceway, though the comings and goings were constant. It must be small, or curtained: long creepers with wide, interlacing leaves hanging down to conceal the hole. But there was no rustle, no whisper of fronds.

Her body was in water, a thin rubber sheath between her skin and the cold wet. But it was warm. A hot spring? She moved gently with the ripples;

must be a breakwater nearby fencing off the sick bay, away from the main thoroughfare. The oldwoman hand came to her out of the water. Frogwomen not rockwomen. The first generation to develop gills.

Pain again, churning and red hot pokers. She was alone in a furnace burning, until the hand returned, insisted.

"Where do you come from?"

Scimitel saw the city with its enormous glass buildings, the broken white line down the middle of the road, between the lanes of a two-way street. She was walking along the line, had to keep moving because it was only wide enough for one foot at a time. At the end of each line, usually four paces, she must jump the tarmac to the next line. If she fell to right or left, the cars would crush her; if a careless toe or heel strayed over the straight and narrow, it would be sliced off by the next wheel. Every now and then, when she was exhausted, there was an island in the road where she could sleep. The cars roared past and the people behind kept on inexorably; as soon as the time came, she must get to her feet and set off again. It was cruel to call them islands. At the end came the roundabout where cars sped round in circles till they could reach their exit. Then you must throw yourself into the maelstrom, swim your lungs out to the central reservation. Either the cars claimed you or you reached a haven of benches, grass and an ornamental lake.

"From the city," said Zay, in the rubber sack next to her. "Sleek glass towers, everything sparkling, hosed out before day. I'm a performer. I wear lurex one-ply and I skate, conducting the traffic. My peak was an entrechat dix executed on four chevrons separating two lanes of cars. No one can entrechat dix, but I did. No glorious accident of early morning, first up and alone, practising in empty streets, but at full tilt of rush hour, citizens hanging off the backs of buses, faces crowding into office windows way above me. I had springs in my skates and I leapt – for the secret is

124

to leap high enough, anyone can entrechat in an armchair – the zibus was swinging overhead, the travelator crossing the aerial section, the highway one mass traffic jam, and all the lifts in all the glass towers stopped to watch. I took their breath away. For ten seconds I held the breath and heartbeat of the city."

Why wasn't she there now? Traitor. One who belongs may come and go. A foreigner can never leave. "I am from the city," Zay announced firmly, allowing no doubts.

Ithaca saw the Benaccar Residence: one hundred sixteen zappers and herself, strongest swimmer, best at shotput, fast runner, good climber, fifty per cent higher maths score than anyone in her year. The new educator, shocked that a nelly had infiltrated the most prestigious zapper residence, announced that nellies took too long drying their hair afterwards to play cricket, that it wrenched their insides to put the shot, and that their anatomy caused them to urinate in swimming pools. Competition disqualified; the zappers applauded. Ithaca stood up after father's assembly, "You've been sitting in a pool of blood," said Athos, pointing to the seat of her apparel. She alone had been picked out for this curse. She wanted no womb to plague her, no breasts to declare the plague, and, though she had no other use for it, she wanted a tube between her legs, with valve, so she could be trusted to go swimming as before. Instead, she defied them, too late to turn her into a woman. Every night she swam, back and forth, underwater, dolphin, butterfly, crawl, twenty times, a hundred times. Her father loved her best because she was the strongest, the cleverest. She was his, nelly though she was, and nothing he could do was wrong: a triumphant Benaccar exception. He fired the educator and her lessons continued.

"I am my father's daughter."

The water lapped and sucked greedily at the rubber sheaths.

"What happened?" Ithaca asked the others.

Throats were cleared; air indrawn, sighed out; lips smacked.

"There's someone in here," whispered Ithaca.

"The rockwomen. The fishwomen. The rockwomen." Like windscreen wipers in driving rain, the hand allowed Scimitel tormented attempts at clarity. Somewhere two stones beat a simple rhythm, as though scanning a line of poetry, or teaching a foreigner the stress of an unfamiliar word. Ithaca writhed, struggling to escape the sheath, succeeded only in admitting an uncomfortable trickle of water, warm as an eye bath.

"Can either of you see anything?" she asked.

Again the stones beat rhythmically, followed by tuts, clicks, air vibrating between lip and tongue. Reluctantly, with the courage of one who seals her fate by saving her companions, Zay flapped the tip of her tongue against the back of her tooth ridge, blowing air in an even stream, glad of the cover of darkness. "Maggot mouth", "maggot mouth"; the cries had followed her into the cave. They had squatted in wait, knowing that sooner or later she would give in, revert to nature, and talk the language of her ancestors with its characteristic grimaces, its lightning changes of expression where the mouth moves so quickly the lips resemble twin maggots writhing in the skull. From all over tongues flapped and clicked their reply.

"Ithaca," Zay said, once the flapping and trilling had quieted and she'd had time to ponder, "Who are the Obsolescent?"

"No idea."

"They want to know if we were sent by the Obsolescent."

"You speak Tramontane," Ithaca stated flatly. An iron grill thundered down between them.

"I do," Zay apologised, "But not well. I've forgotten a lot." She trilled back to whoever was in the cavern. The reply was immediate but, as before, the sounds seemed to her so distorted it was only after she repeated them in her own mouth that she realised what was meant. She could hardly bear to relay it, though she might as well go on now.

"They think I may have, that the translation, that possibly I translated them wrong."

Already she was slipping into the crevasse between the two languages, her careful assimilation eroding under the almost familiarity of the old. To learn the language of the city she had stopped speaking, reading, listening or thinking in Tramontane; any thought which could not be formulated urbanely she had banished as best she could: translation was treachery. It made no sense to savour the thousand tastes of city wines rolling across the tongue in a language more accustomed to distinguishing pure water from contaminated. Her inheritance of poverty shamed her, she welcomed the vista of wealth and variety: fifty terms for the consumption of alcohol, more than a hundred for the after-effects. Stupendous.

"The Jubilant?" Zay tried again.

"Don't make yourself ridiculous," said Ithaca, "Do you have some impression how many there are? what they intend to do to us? if anyone's blocking the exit hole?"

"I think they're waiting," said Zay, "I mean, it depends on what we're doing here."

"I came because Soren told me to," snapped Ithaca. The awesome strength which ennobled her above the need to snap and fuss proved frustratingly redundant against the pliant walls of the sheath. Willingly they let in water, but they would not let her out.

At the name of Soren there came a change in the cave.

No one switched the light on to reveal the workings of an ancient and highly developed civilisation; a hall vast as an amphitheatre, the floor, barring a wooden gallery round the circumference, composed of an artificial lake, the heat of which can be attested by the steam rising from its surface; rows of rockwomen in sleeping sheaths which float gently on the ripples. It is not immediately apparent that the rockwomen are

127

each at least one hundred years old, nor that most are blind, nor that these women, finding three strangers in a state of collapse brought on by an overdose of moss, have carried them to the lying-in bay for the strongest antidote available, the rockwomen's panacea: fourteen days of sleep.

The name of Soren does not bring instant recognition to the rockwomen. For example, they do not realise with a drumbeat and a roll of thunder that the big stranger has been sent to the Scrub to allow her lover to convalesce in peace; nor that the Tramontane who speaks the language of a hundred years ago has come only to win back her beloved; nor that the little one is a presumptuous adventuress who should be spanked and reported to her father.

The citizens know only that they have begun to feel better, that they are helped out of the sheaths and onto dry land, that they are fed substances warm, bland and nourishing.

The rockwomen know only that Soren has never yet tried to harm them, that the Senectity is concerned with the survival of oldwomen, that some, even, of the rockwomen present can trace their own paths along the refugee line from the city.

A great splash and murmur begins as more and more of the rockwomen awake, pull themselves in to shore, and prepare to resume work. Their half hour is up. With elaborate courtesy they invite the strangers to speak with them in the moss fields, the spores must be culled if the dusk is not to be wasted. There follows a shuffling of slow feet, an encouragement of pats. When they creep out through a low, vine-covered doorway and emerge into twilight, it is hard for the three strangers to believe that the stooped, squat figures, with skin coarse as sandstone are the ones they have come to find. Scimitel stares at them, as frankly as she might a noted landmark, unable to leave each face until she has spotted its eyes, nose and mouth. The eyes are most frequently absent and the first thing she seeks. Sockets are of anatomical comfort only. How is it possible to speak to a person who has no eyes? Ithaca is impatient as Scimitel is curious. Zay is shocked, ashamed to have revealed any linguistic connection between such creatures and herself, but the rockwomen are insistent that she translate an explanation.

"Once there were three rockwomen and they shared one eye between them, passing it from sister to sister. One day, as the first sister plucked the eye from her socket to hand to the second sister, a stranger snatched it, hoping the women would fight. But they were more relieved than angry; seeing had been an irksome duty distracting them from more immediate senses."

"Some women would thank you for hitting them sooner than admit it hurt," scoffed Ithaca. "Or have you got the translation wrong again?"

"No," said Scimitel, "I've heard that story before. From my nursemaid."

"What's the matter, Ithaca," said Zay, "Can't cope without the authority of strength?"

But it was the sight of those grey granite faces, those shrivelled humps of bodies which turned Ithaca's stomach, and she the lover of an oldwoman. Surrounded by mobile ruins.

"Shapeless," she muttered, turning away.

Scimitel caught the mutter with surprise. Her own flat body seemed shapeless beside the complex folds of the rockwomen. She watched fascinated as they tended and picked the moss, raising delicate pads to their faces, sorting and grading to some unknown standard. Their fingers were so swift and steady it was hard to believe their eyes were sightless.

"What are they doing with the moss like that if they can't see?" she asked Zay.

"Taste outside the body," said Zay automatically. "Doesn't exist in the city, but in the Scrub you can taste anything by putting it to your nose and breathing in." It made sense; that's how she knew there were plants covering the cavern entrance, thought Scimitel, but . . .

"Sometimes the wind carries the taste. You can trace fires ten miles away," Zay added.

"Teach me Tramontane," Scimitel pleaded.

"No," Zay shrugged.

Ithaca strode off into the moss beds to demand answers. Zay made to follow.

"Leave her," Scimitel advised, "She won't want to be humiliated in front of you." Zay grinned and climbed with Scimitel to the grass mound overlooking the lake. At that distance the oldwomen were again indistinguishable from rocks; Ithaca resembled a geologist doubled over her specimens.

Scimitel listened carefully to the sounds the rock-women made, carried up from the lake on the breeze. She tried to isolate a 'yes' or a 'no', words which would be said often and might stand alone. But each speech was so long, so quick, so intricate. Not only did she often fail to notice where one speaker left off and another took up, but she could not always say which sounds were speech, which throat clearing and nose blowing.

"At least tell me 'yes' and 'no'," she urged, dragging Zay back from a dream of the city.

Zay had dreamed so often of the city when she lived beneath it, and still it never failed to excite. She had learned it. A system made by man you could get to the end of, not like this green hollow. She was skating in the dark in a burn-out park at the back of a crenellated restaurant. The flowers and trees were grey, a low city hum in her ears, when suddenly the lawn flooded with light, the flowers burst into colour, peacocks shrieked and flew in clumsy bustles onto the wall and a bell was sounded from the restaurant. Now she skated in a spotlight as the diners poured outside and the peacocks fanned their marvellous tails. Now she zipped and zigzagged around standstill traffic queueing bumper to bumper for a space in the multistorey. Emboldened by her leaps along their running boards and fenders, she swept up onto the car roofs and skated her triumphal progress over the drivers' heads.

"There is no 'yes' or 'no'," she said, irritably. "Only Tramontanes understand Tramontane. It doesn't have the on-off switch of Urbanity."

"No electric current?" suggested Scimitel eagerly.

"Exactly," said Zay, pleased despite herself. "You know how energy from gas, wind, water, solar, nuclear power is transformed into electricity for touch-of-the button use? Cheaper and cleaner in the short term and much quicker. Ithaca weighed present speed against long-term pollution and exhaustion; accorded speed the priority. Urbane language works the same way: speed of communication whatever the later cost. A thing is only this because it isn't that. Urbane thinkers ask themselves at each stage, like a flow diagram, is this plus or minus male, plus or minus citizen, plus or minus young? The guiding principle of the process is death. Why so few meanings? Why such short paths? Because you might die next minute your message unsaid. Plus or minus only works in a state of perpetual crisis where it is reasonable to screen out other options."

"But we kept vocabulary books to record all the words for sex, for drugs, for drink," objected Scimitel, "There are hundreds of options."

"There are lots of words to describe, or euphemise, death," Zay retorted.

"Drugs, drink, they sound like exits," Scimitel agreed, "But sex? Sex is . . . "

"What do you know about it?"

"Everything: loss of self; union with the whole; male female fusion . . . "

"Did you say loss?"

"It's meant to work that way, I know. But with the other nellies I felt more selfconscious," Scimitel confessed.

"Increased self-consciousness with nellies is not what the city means by sex," said Zay.

"You were going to tell me how Tramontane's

different from all that," Scimitel reminded her.

Something didn't fit. Zay felt caught in a lie. Like Scimitel she had learned the city's wealth in its lexicon: to drink, to be a drinker, to be drunk, to be a drunk, to have one's first drunk, to have one's first drink. Drunk as a skunk, drunk as a pig, drunk as a sow, drunk as a stoat, drunk as an owl. Dead drunk. What did that mean save that any animal, extinct as far as the city knew for its citizens had never laid eyes on them, could be returned to life and remembrance by simple comparison with the gait of a drunkard? That was wealth? Or the ubiquitous, multifarious 'it'. Can't get enough of it. Smile if you had it last night. Pop it in a bag time. Any substantive could stand for a penis, any verb for penetration. Expansion or reduction? Two ways to read any utterance. Yet one spoke also of scarcity, of the limited resources of the city.

"You promised," said Scimitel.

"Tramontane," said Zay consideringly, "is different."

"Yes?" Scimitel encouraged her.

"It's, the basis, I mean the purpose is different. It starts from an ideal of dignity and the guiding principle is life. It's not that Tramontanes believe they'll never die, but that life is more important. Our words are not built around open graves. The better, the closer we, I mean they, understand, the higher the quality of life. Conversation throws up questions, replies give the conditions under which a positive answer could be given."

"Can't you bear to disagree?"

"They disagree all the time and all night long. My mother and her friend . . . "

"A woman?" asked Scimitel eagerly.

Zay looked at Scimitel. "Male Trams aren't allowed inside the compounds of the city." Scimitel blushed a deep pink, disappearing into the sunset behind her.

"Ithaca introduces womb surrender. My mother thinks it a good thing. Her friend thinks it's bad. But they argue about human dignity, women's dignity. My mother says inequality damages women's dignity, the inequality should be removed. Her friend agrees about the damage, disagrees about the cure."

"All night?"

"All their lives," Zay replied. "What you hear in the clicks and hisses of the rockwomen are the subtleties and tones of all their arguments. Though I think they simplify for me."

Ithaca bellowed at them to come down; she needed Zay to translate.

"Plenty of rest, good diet, fresh air and exercise."

Ithaca attempted patience.

"You could try moss, but you won't be able to carry enough back with you to make a difference."

There was a secret. Soren had sent her to find the secret. Moss was commonplace.

"High up in the mountains where the air is trapped in the valleys and the sun scorches, you will find moss in flower. Tiny delicate flowers which blow their seed away on the wind. You must wait till evening to cull them. During the day the pods are tight closed and drenched with sap, but when the heat passes off the pods open and then the seeds are fit. One handful of dry seeds will last a year. Collect as many handfuls as the years you want Karlin to live."

"How do we know where to look?"

"Climb, keep climbing till you begin to hear the lego-firons. They lie half-stunned, basking on flat rocks, the sun on their backs, hot stone on their stomachs, but they'll feel you coming by the vibrations of your foot-steps and scurry away into the ferns. As you walk you'll hear the noise of claw on quartz. The track is precipitous but you'll smell the trees we burnt to mark the path. Once you're through the ferns and into the open, there'll be a breeze. It clears away the burnt smell and swamps you with resin. Can't miss it. Just before you reach the treeline you'll cross a stream. There's moss there too, but it never quite dries out. Follow the stream to its source, you'll feel the earth get harder and you can smell moss flowers through anything."

"But we won't recognise it."

"Watch out for a new smell. One you haven't smelt before. Minty with a hint of aniseed."

Mint, aniseed, legofirons, smell . . . it made no sense to Ithaca. Either Zay was making it up or the rockwomen were trying to trick them.

"What does it look like?" Ithaca asked firmly.

"You tell us."

"What about the moss at the water's edge," Ithaca asked cunningly, "Why can't we cut that?"

"Too concentrated; you wouldn't know what doses to give. Besides, it belongs to us. We cultivated it. The scorched valley is a long way to go."

"They're trying to get rid of us," Ithaca whispered, as though the rockwomen understood Urbanity, "Moss doesn't have flowers."

"It's not really moss," Zay explained, "They use our words to be polite. Among themselves they call it tchai."

Ithaca stared at Zay.

After two hours in the mossbeds the rockwomen gathered their tools, stored the day's harvest in a silo above the cavern and got back into their sleeping sheaths.

"They sleep for half an hour every two hours," Zay explained.

"Excellent," said Ithaca. "We're going to grab as much of those moss spores as we can carry and head for the mountains. They've as good as said they couldn't come after us."

"No," said Scimitel, "You go. I'm staying."

"You can't stay," said Zay, "You're at least one hundred years younger than the youngest of the rockwomen. What happens when you start your period and no one else has had one for a century?"

"I risk worse than incomprehension if I start in the city. If I go with you, either I'll die on the way or I'll get eaten when we arrive. I am not going back."

"What will you do here?" asked Ithaca curiously.

"Grow up and grow old," said Scimitel.

"The rockwomen haven't invited you," Zay objected, angry that anyone should speak ill of her city but herself.

"I'll risk their displeasure." Scimitel pointed to the mountains with their white peaks and purple haze. "I cannot climb those. I am too small and my arms are too short and too weak. Ithaca would have to carry me, and then she would drop me."

"There isn't room on my back for Scimitel and the moss," said Ithaca. But she was loth to leave the little blue-veined creature with those aged rocks, the nelly deserved her youth, not life among the ruins.

Twentieth Sighting: UPTURNED PALMS

Ithaca luxuriated. The granite was firm and steadfast; the moss spores, tied tightly to her back, did not bump against her as she jumped from rock to rock. No longer an overgrowth, she was nimble as a chamois, natural as an avalanche. She dived up the mountain with a spring of relief, a beached whale returning to water. Leaving Zay hundreds of feet below, Ithaca was alone, accepted with the same generous challenge thrown to legofiron, proteus or goat. Unused in the valley, her muscles responded with the alert enthusiasm of unleashed hunting dogs. As she bent, ran two paces and leapt onto a higher boulder, landing knees braced with confident balance, she revelled in the strength and co-ordination which never left her. She could do it, she could do it still, after weeks of inactivity. Other climbers used ropes, but, with arms upstretched, she spanned twelve feet. The views were stark as the dusk turned to night and she paused a second from testing the stability of a crag to gaze at the giants around her. Up the next chimney she would find a flat stretch to spend the night. Though she loved climbing in the dark, she did not expect Zay to share her excitement.

Zay was a long way down, toiling like an ant. From

where Ithaca stood the gradient of Zay's climb was not apparent, she could as well have been walking on the flat. She stumbled and crawled, like a toddler on a tablecloth, an actor miming an ascent. It was comic, always, to see the response without the cause. Ithaca breathed in, watched a slow drift of smoke rise up the valley, a bird swoop from the rocks, plummet a hundred feet and plunge its beak into the neck of a smaller bird, clasp its prey in its claws and carry it off to a private place. A feather fell a little way, then lifted on an updraught. So much you could learn about the valley watching the movements in empty air. Safer here watching than asking. Ithaca sat cross-legged on her perch and no one stared at her enormous thighs, and no one asked was she a woman or a man.

At last Zay appeared, crawling up the chimney, elbows back against one wall, knees pushing against the other.

"Not like that," Ithaca called, "If you slip you've got no back up."

Zay didn't move. It was best to learn from your own body and the give and take of the rock. Broken bones are, however, an expensive lesson.

"I'm coming down," shouted Ithaca.

Zay would not be pleased to have instruction forced upon her, but her ascent was so reckless Ithaca was certain she would fall. In two neat movements Ithaca had climbed below her.

"Put your left foot on this spur."

Zay's response was to let go completely. She slumped into Ithaca's arms. As the sudden weight hit her Ithaca fell backwards, grabbing Zay as an automatic reflex. Together they slithered to the bottom of the chimney.

At last Ithaca had come for her. Zay was delighted when Ithaca strode off up the mountain; she was able to climb at her own pace, clamber over rocks too frail for Ithaca's weight. It was easy and fun and she liked to pant, feel sweat and be rewarded with a different view every step. Ithaca rushed for the top, did not savour the route. Then it got steeper and the grass so

138

slippery you had to keep to the rocks. There was so much up. Nowhere to put your hands or feet and the ledges so narrow she'd been thrown over backwards by the weight of the moss she was carrying. She began to feel sick at the thought of moving another step and not knowing if her foot would slip. Only not being able to stay where she was kept her moving onward. There was no safe foothold within reach; she would have had to pull herself to the next ledge by her arms. But she was a skater, her arms served a purely ornamental function, only her legs had real muscle. She moved onto the knobble of rock she had already tested and decided was not stable. If she scrambled fast enough onto the next foothold, perhaps the knobble would not notice her passing. It was not the knobble which gave way but the foothold after it which she'd had no time to test. She fell only a few feet but the jagged surface ripped through her one-ply, her hands and thighs were covered with short, deep cuts. She had long abandoned Ithaca's ackademickal as too heavy and dangerous: it trapped the wind inside it, billowed out like a balloon and threatened to blow her off the rockface. Her hands smarted with pain as she struggled upward; by the time she reached the chimney they were so swollen she could not grip with them at all but concertinaed herself between the two walls from elbow to knee. It did not work. She felt herself sliding back, each time sliding back.

"Sit down," said Ithaca's calm voice, "Right here. There's room for both of us."

Dazed and whimpering, Zay sat. Ithaca disappeared from her side and returned with some lengths of wet cloth. She dabbed and cleaned the cuts, then bound them.

"There's a shallow pool higher up," she explained.

She took no advantage of Zay's state to continue her side of their quarrel.

"I'm sorry I took off and left you," she said, "I thought we'd both prefer it, and I did watch to make sure you were alright."

"You're so noble," said Zay.

"I expect you're being sarcastic," Ithaca replied, "but I mean to be noble."

"You are good."

"Don't be grateful. You hurt your hands, you got scared. I came down to help.

"Why wouldn't you help Scimitel?"

"Are we chatting to calm your nerves?"

"I want to know."

"She reminds me of Athos. When we were little once Benaccar took us away on a trip to the hinterland. It was Athos he wanted, I was a smoke-screen. We had arrived and Benaccar went to check the water levels. Athos turned to me.

'I don't want to, Ithaca.'

Such a look on his face. I was his sister, his twin, and he looked at me with complete confidence, unquestioning trust.

'But you do it with the zappers.'

'It's different among us.'

He knew I'd have a plan, so I had one. We took food for three days and we hid on the mountain. It was our mountain, we climbed all over it on gym afternoons. Benaccar didn't find us till morning. We saw him climbing up towards us. He looked at Athos.

'I see you have spirit,' he said. 'That's good. I won't break your spirit.'

Athos nudged me and Benaccar finished.

'But never let me learn that you borrowed it from your sister.'

"Did he ever find out?" asked Zay.

"No," said Ithaca. "But the thought terrified Athos. He did not know what was meant. I was in the smoking room polishing trophies. Benaccar had a cheroot, a zapper knelt in front of him, palms upturned. It was Parris, Athos' replacement. Benaccar knocked the ash from his cheroot into Parris' hands; Parris crossed the room and threw the ash in the bin. I went to Athos and we watched through the door. Then he understood.

'It's not the ash, is it,' he said, 'That ash isn't hot. It's making Parris feel small.'"

"Scimitel has more spirit than your brother will ever have," said Zay.

"He died a good death."

The words of a true citizen. Zay felt the Tramontane in her revolt against a city which waited for death to tell them how they had lived.

"He left Benaccar to return to the Scrub and become a freedom fighter. How he could go back to where he'd never been, I do not know."

Zay knew.

"He was Secretary to their President. We call him the Dictator; Athos called him the President. They flew to a conference with the city fathers in the hinterland, and someone planted a bomb in the plane. It exploded mid-flight. Athos died right above the mountain where we spent the night."

"Do you know who did it?"

"The whole thing: Benaccar, Athos, Parris, the freedom fight and the President, they're all an affair between men. Only the mountain and I are still alive. Parris did it. He has since been forcibly retired."

"Ithaca, I never know when you're being ironic."

"Perhaps they got me too and only the mountain is left."

"Why didn't you join Athos?"

"You know what they do to perverts in the Scrub."

"How could I? Assimilated Trams are forbidden to read about zurban life."

"From my privileged position I have learned quite enough. In the Scrub a respectable woman is married to a man and breeds his sons. A woman alone is a tramp, two women together are perverts, three women is a brothel and they all get rounded up every twelfth, kept in prison until claimed by father or husband. Unclaimed women are sent to marriage stations up north where there is no food, no water and no way out. Respectable women are as respected as married women anywhere."

141

"There are city women living in the Scrub," Zay remarked.

"And every now and then they round up one of them and shove her in a prison cell, and that's the only way we hear about the rest of them."

"I don't hear about any of it," Zay snapped, "Unless my Status Six lover bothers to let me know."

Ithaca was not Zay's lover. She was Karlin's.

"I didn't hear about Athos either," said Ithaca, "not for ages. I knew the President's plane had exploded and I was sure Athos was on it. I scanned all the newspapers, tuned all the broadcasts, but because they were only Tramontanes, they didn't get given names. Until at the bottom of a triumph piece about the tram leadership turmoil it noted, 'A'thos A'ccar, President O'chel's Secretary, is reported to have been aboard the aircraft . . . '"

It was now completely dark, though at this latitude and in this season, it would remain so only a few hours. Ithaca stood across the mouth of the chimney, clasped her hands together forming a platform for Zay to stand on. She lifted her slowly up the rockface to a ridge which jutted out a good six inches. Once Zay was steady, Ithaca climbed round her to point out the next foothold. So on until, a few feet from the top, Ithaca pulled herself over the ledge and reached down to swing Zay up.

"It's one of the few occasions when I take uncomplicated pride in my body," said Ithaca.

"You walk with arrogance," said Zay, "Every stride says 'I am better than a woman'."

Zay had never seen knees the like of Ithaca's. The first time her lover undressed Zay expected biceps, triceps and sharply defined pectorals. Knees she thought were always rounded bone but Ithaca's were divided into sinewy sections, you could see the muscles stretching and contracting like an anatomy diagram.

"I don't understand why women make such a parade of feebleness. They could be strong and proud of it," said Ithaca.

142

"We didn't start with your advantages."

"But the muscles you see on me are muscles every woman has. I've been using mine and they do not use theirs."

"You had a father who pushed and cheered you every step. Other nellies are ridiculed at the first sign of brawn."

"Look at Scimitel, taught to run with roped ankles, and with roped ankles she ran away. Look at you, Zay. Born under the city but you skated to the top. Some of them, their spirit's broken before they're born. The books they write, revelling in bruises because it makes them righteous. They scorn my strength and my love for them as unwomanly, call me worse than a man. They have the protection of the law of the fathers; I have no rights but the ones I fight for."

"The rights you fight for? The right of a woman to have her womb removed."

"Let's stop arguing and go to sleep."

"I'll go to sleep," Zay replied, the Tramontane rising in her, "But I will never stop arguing."

Twenty First Sighting: THE FIRST FIFTY YEARS

The rockwomen argued all night about the little one. They would argue about her all their lives. They said they should take her into the mountains and leave her to fend for herself. They said that they could not bear to be the ones to do it. They said they must either live with their consciences, or they must live with the little one. They said they should take her to the refugee camps. They said she was a refugee. They said that according to the rules she must stay in a camp till she reached a hundred. They said they must not make her an exception. They said that she was an exception. They said that life was hard in the camps and the inmates were bitter. They said the inmates had only questioned the ways of the city once it threatened their lives. They said the inmates had enjoyed the city and polluted themselves. They said the camps were there to allow citizens to evacuate poisons from their system. They said the little one had spent few years in the city, had been given no choice and no benefits. They said the camps were not a punishment but a decontamination unit and the little one had not had time to become contaminated. They said that she had already discovered her sense of smell.

They said they did not want another sighted person,

it was too much of a liability. They said sight could be useful if properly supervised; the little one could help rubber-weld the submarines. They said that the little one, like themselves, would not remain sighted long; she would begin to rely on the finer senses. They said they could not be sure of this; she was very young, hardly born, and they had scant experience of persons her age. They said that it would be an experiment and they might learn. They said it could not be an experiment; if the little one was accepted, she must stay with them. They said this was all very well, but they did not want to take charge of her, they were busy with the grown-ups.

"I'll do the first fifty years," said one, finally.

Twenty Second Sighting: CONVERSATION WITH A FEMALE STRANGER

The shadows had solidified into recognisable blocks.
That flat plane stretching before her was the bed,
those corrugations the folds and wrinkles of the
blanket. She wiggled her foot and the blanket moved.
Power. Over there, where the light was so strong it
hurt her eyes, was the window, and, rattling slightly,
the curtain. Karlin practised looking from the window
to the bed and back; it took so long to focus and
refocus that everything was followed by a trail of
shooting stars. She began to take exact measure of her
world: the weight and ply of the coverlet, the varied
colours of the curtain, steel blue as it left the wall,
green and sun-blistered in the middle, the last shutter
rusted by rain on an ill-fitting window; muffled traffic
and distant hoverpods; the humming of the pater noster,
disembodied voices from other floors. She could roll
to the edge of the bed, buoyed by adventure, lever
herself against the wall, put her cold feet into slippers,
lean forward till she held the griprail of the zimmer,
and go and close the curtain.

It was exciting to glance at the floor from the height
of her own standing body, spot a small, dark object
and, after some concentration, declare it to be a
hairbrush even though her queasy balance would

mean ten minutes' effort to pick it up, and her wasted arms would require again as much to pull it through her hair. Either she would walk to the window and close the curtains, or she would pick up the hair brush. But, within easy reach of her left arm was the open doorway of her bedroom, offering the irresistible temptation to visit her own flat.

For so long oldwomen on the rota had appeared and disappeared through that door, bearing fresh water, the day's puree, a confession which required a silent listener. They sat on the bed, patted Karlin's hand to make sure they had her attention, were careful to speak within her tunnel of vision. Karlin was a thin, shallow riverbed, smelly and stagnant (the first odour to reach her nose after years of olfactory loss was the stench of her own body), she was stretched along a line of surface tension upon which a thousand insects laid their eggs. She would hatch out into a million flies, a million worms. Little did the rota know but the river to which they entrusted their secrets would not remain long confined, soon she would overflow her banks, rush down the valley and thunder their stories to the world. They were sorry they had used her work and had not thanked her. They were sorry they had used her work and had not credited her. They were sorry they had kicked her as an all-powerful person deserves to be kicked, since she was no longer all-powerful. They were sorry they had credited Soren for their rescue from the wreckage when it had been Karlin who crept into the well night after night to leave them food and courage. They were sorry. They were not sorry. Only on her deathbed could they forgive her for having done exactly what was needed.

The bedroom door opened onto a short passage leading to the toilet. Karlin had attempted it that morning with Soren. The passage was narrow, she could place a hand on each wall and guide herself along. When she stumbled, she bumped rather than fell against the wall. Soren felt each bump coming,

148

but stood resolutely behind Karlin, hoping to avoid even the suggestion of reins.

There were small pools of sunlight on the living room carpet and the breeze cast rippling shadows on the white walls. Karlin held onto the doorframe and feasted on the sight. Each drab old precious object sat in waiting. They believed in her recovery. Not their fault the armchair was too high and too far, the carpet too slippery. Karlin lifted the front of the zimmer, pushed it forward and shuffled into its embrace. She fixed her eyes on the vertical line down the side of the window; because of the confusion in her right ear, her balance rested in her sight. There were twenty steps to cover in the crossing to the armchair. She hoped not to fall, but if she fell, then she would get up again. When she had completed the twentieth step, held firm to the arm of the chair, swung the zimmer to one side but within reach, as she had practised, she looked into the basket at the back of the frame for the hairbrush, and realised she had left it on the bed. It did not matter. She had walked twenty steps today and she'd walk another twenty before she went to bed. Meanwhile the shadows of the leaves chased each other across the ceiling and the armchair was slowly becoming engulfed in sunlight. Her mind no longer the one spark in a vegetable body, Karlin basked in the armchair she had walked to, the slippers she had put on her feet, the objects her own eyes could pick out and her tongue name.

Karlin soon tired of being glad. The rota had kept her alive when they could so easily have killed her. They could so easily have poisoned her with food she could not eat; left their own sickbeds to tend her, passed on germs she had not strength to withstand. But they had been serious, sensible and devoted. It had not been easy for them. Gleaning food for one was a nightly occupation without the extra needs of an invalid. The Tramontanes shovelled mountains of ejected but nourishing waste into the transporters and out of reach. Karlin had been adept at bargaining for it: two bales of fruit for a course in computers, a keg of akyan for basic literacy. The rubbish strike made life, momentarily, easier for oldwomen as the waste remained on permanent display. Karlin had taken an onlooker's interest in the story, a touchstone of her interest in the world.

They had wanted her out of the way, in hospital. Perhaps they liked the neat orderliness of hospital visiting where they could sit and knit and leave when they dropped a stitch, where the staff, not the patient decide when a visit is welcome. Easier to be turned away by medical imperative than the invalid's distaste. That was what Karlin blamed them for; she liked her resentment to be accurate. They had ceased believing she knew best, had tried to break her. Desde had wept beside the bed, Karlin's wasted hand in hers and sobbed.

"You were our foremother."

Surely Karlin had not recovered on fury alone. The bitterness of that one, foolish remark had filled her with such rage, could one confuse it with the will to live? At her weakest she had not heeded any of them, kind or foolish, but begun the necessary preparations for leaving, only she had not left.

Loud, lame footsteps came out of the lift and stopped at Karlin's flat door. Someone knocked. It could not be anyone on rota, they still had keys and were accustomed to letting themselves in. Ithaca? Let it be Ithaca the Enormous, swooping down from the hinterland, pulling up in her silver Quantum, striding through the flat to reclaim her lover. Karlin had been outraged by Ithaca's sexual presence when she needed all she had for herself. Had she not explained and serviced Ithaca's emotions long enough? Now, with the warm sun and the light-show Karlin felt a sharp pang of longing.

"Who is it?"

"Me, dear, Essa. I've come to take you to the meeting."

"What meeting?"

150

"Why the Senectity. You *are* out of touch."

Did Karlin detect triumph in Essa's voice?

"I can't walk that far."

"Not to worry. I've brought you a present."

Essa's eyes sparkled achievement. It had been hard to find, hard to remove and hard to manoeuvre into Karlin's building. But it would make the difference, and Karlin would not want to miss the meeting.

Karlin waited in the armchair.

"Close your eyes."

Karlin closed them. It was restful after the battery of light. There was some huffing and puffing, banging, opening of doors and dragging.

"Look."

Karlin looked. She saw the object of her worst fears gleaming before her, confirmed by Essa's smiling encouragement. As though someone had thrust a mirror to her face without warning and without discussion. As though, preening herself on her returning strength, imagining her lover lifting her in adoring arms, Karlin had been forced to see how the lines of pain had etched themselves across her forehead and around her eyes and know that she would never pass as young again. Her once sharp chin was now lost in the loose skin of her neck; her hair turned white overnight; her arms, once smooth and round, now were sticks with loose skin flapping like wet laundry. These changes Karlin had catalogued, painfully, for herself. Then she had known that Ithaca would never want her again. She had berated Ithaca in absentia for being as shallow as Karlin had always expected.

Karlin turned her head away, denying the appropriateness of the shining object which dominated her living room. How dare Essa take advantage like this? Such effort she must have made to be so accurately cruel.

"Splendid, isn't it? Strong too."

"Go away," Karlin cried, "This is beneath you."

"I thought you might take it like this but it will come in very useful."

"It's bad enough losing my face without slumping in a wheelchair."

"We all look our age, Karlin," Essa said more gently, "And you've helped make that easier. The wheelchair is a present without sarcasm to make your life easier. Until you can walk again."

"I can walk."

Essa waited until Karlin's tears abated.

"You can walk a few steps, then you get tired and overbalance. If you sat in the chair, I could push you all over the city. You wouldn't have to wait for reports on the Senectity and the food supply."

"Maybe you meant well, Essa, but they raised the kerb to get rid of wheelchairs . . . "

"It's risky for any of us to venture out these days. Though you used to pass more often than most. I would only wheel you in the small hours when the young are in bed and oldwomen roam the streets."

"Basketcase. I'd be an old basket. I'd rather not leave my flat until I can walk out on my own two legs."

"Lot of oldwomen in the Senectity use wheelchairs. Look, I've brought you the leaflet about the meeting."

"The Senectity will be meeting at 3am on the 16th in the footstools of the Ackademy. We urge every oldwoman to come, or tune in her screen if she has one, as we have urgent matters to discuss. None of you can be unaware of the increasing number of attacks caused by the Tramontane dispute and the absence of the city Ideo . . .

All papers should be in by 3am on the 15th to allow a full 24 hours for transcription.

Signers available.

Full access. Wheelchairs welcome. Help provided."

"That's what you can do with your wheelchair, Essa," Karlin sobbed, "Take it to the Senectity meeting. I'm sure they'll make it most welcome."

How easy it was for an individual to become at war

with the community. Karlin had been at the first murmurings of the Senectity, now it had joined the enemy, the throng which would get rid of weakness by ridding itself of the weak.

"It's poorly phrased, Karlin," said Essa the pacifier, "You must go and tell them off about it. A wheelchair can be a step up as well as down. If you are used to running about like a young thing, and life in a wheelchair means never skiing again, well that is a tragedy. But if you've been too weak to sit up and eat, the strength to use a wheelchair is a great achievement."

Karlin stored Essa's "the strength to use a wheelchair is a great achievement" alongside Desde's "You were our foremother" and Malachi's "I think you're dying. Oh, I can't bear it." But, on the long walks she used to take into the hinterland, years ago when citizenship protected youngwomen from assault by male Tramontanes, Karlin had coped with her fear of dogs by approaching them directly: "Come here, you brute. You wouldn't want to bite me. There, that's better." She had not paused to store memories of gnashing teeth and panting tongues. Those walks had lasted hours, all day sometimes, and she had watched the women on the mountain, in the fields and rivers as she watched city women on the streets and travelators. She watched them, women whose names she did not know, women she would never meet again, and she saw how they helped each other with young ones, bundles, water, songs and kindness. Sometimes there was a conversation with a female stranger, a treasure to mull over. She formed an idea of female goodness. She started the Senectity because she was old and so many youngwomen seemed incurable in their generation gap, but it could as well have been a movement for all women. Surely now, with all her years, she should be behaving better than a young thing. She was not one to turn from a snapping dog, nor turn for long from women. If the capacity to remain recognisably herself had kept her alive in sickness, she would

153

not become a stranger now at the first difficulty.

"Let's go," she said to Essa, raising her arms to be helped into the wheelchair, "And thank you."

Twenty Third Sighting: 'GIVE ME MY PITY BACK'

Were they disappointed she was still alive? Had they prepared their life oration for the body of their dead foremother? A heroine in a wheelchair is no heroine at all. Karlin had ample time to watch reactions: every oldwoman they met kept her eyes fixed on Essa, glancing only briefly downward to see if the chair were occupied, flinching and steeling when they saw that it was. As beachcombers collecting shells flinch to discover a soft-bodied mollusc still in occupation.

The slope of the trade tunnel to the footstools of the Ackademy was so steep at the L bend that Essa feared she would not be able to hold the wheelchair. It gave her a guilty pleasure – all pleasure made Essa feel guilty – to be the power behind the wheel. She thought of the Tramontane nursemaids walking their charges in the burn-out park. Maybe they would never be citizens, but in those prams they pushed the future of the city and only they could still the little citlets' cries. She, Essa, had wheeled E'thane out of the Hall of the Abnormalidads under the nose of the Ackademy. E'thane was crook cracky crazy, better off strapped down and shut away, but it pleased Essa to cock a snook at authority. Would she have been less eager to help Karlin had there not been rumours of a coup? Essa was not so juvenile.

"I could climb down the steps and meet you at the bottom," Karlin suggested. The endless jogging of the wheelchair left her weary and seasick. She wanted to try out her legs on good old-fashioned concrete.

An oldwoman stepped carefully over the trolley tracks, leaning on a wooden cane, breathing hard. When she caught sight of Karlin she stopped still, got a grip on herself and set her face for pity, congratulating her own legs on their sense of purpose.

Holding Essa's arm, Karlin got to her feet and shuffled a dragging pace to the handrail. She stood on the top step, poised for descent into the Senectity. Optimism seized her. Tonight they would listen, pay attention, argue through to a beginning. Portrait of oldwomen trying.

As she watched Karlin clamber out of the chair and walk toward the staircase, the oldwoman's expression changed with the suddenness of summer hail.

"Give me my pity back."

The rage of the innocent caught by the confidence trickster.

Karlin saw, shrugged, resumed her burden.

Twenty Fourth Sighting: SONGS OF CIVIC PRIDE

The computer housing had been transformed from dance floor to conference hall. At the front was installed audio and visual equipment and, unusually, a dais. Upon the dais was a chair, a lectern and a single glass of water. The floor of the hall had been raked so that those situated at the back enjoyed an uncluttered view of the whole proceedings. They bought the view, however, at the cost of their voice which could not be heard from so high up. Only the speaker on the dais enjoyed both view and voice.

As each oldwoman entered the great hall she scanned the horizon, spotted her gang's banner and pushed through the crowd to stand with her kind. The younger members of each group tended toward the front near the dais, the ranks aged as they blended at the back where the seating was placed. Only the back doors were wide enough for wheelchair access thus an ad hoc group formed along the far wall, of diverse opinion, united in their inability to walk, or stand, for long periods, if at all. As though two wheels were politic enough. Lone crazies slunk in corners un-claimed. One stood in an open doorway, staring into the wash of faces. Her own face showed the sharp features of the Tramontane and her wrist was swathed in bandages.

From the back of the hall Karlin picked out those closest in politics to herself. Her eyes bored holes in their craniums until each turned round, recognised her and nodded, getting quietly to their feet a few moments later. Someone tapped Soren's hand. E'thane knew a secret society when she saw one. She started off round the hall to skulk in the shadow of the small group assembling by the oldwoman in the wheelchair.

"Order. Order. We have a proposal that Tessera act as chair. Let's have a vote."

"We do not vote in the Senectity."

"We do not have chairs."

"Only moderators and facilitators."

"To keep our politics moderate and our arguments facile."

Soren bent over to Karlin. "How you doing Rosehips?"

"Right leg's a piece of mahogany from someone's kitchen table and they picked my balance off a helter skelter."

"Small group time?"

"Fewer refugees and more suicides since the Ideo left," said Malachi, "So most of the rooms here are empty."

"Who called the meeting?" asked Karlin.

"Tessera and cohorts. The ones who started the chant: 'Here I stand with my knife in my hand'. They call it a bid for leadership."

Karlin raised an eyebrow without thinking, realised what she'd done and marvelled at the extent to which voluntary movement had returned to her face.

Soren caught amusement of some kind in the air, "Have pity," she laughed, "How can they stage a coup when there's no one to oust?"

"They set us up so they can knock us down," Karlin pursued.

"Maybe they'll feel less virtuous hitting you in that chair," said Desde.

"Maybe it'll make it easier for them," Karlin retorted.

"If we leave now they'll call us elitist," said Malachi.

"Mass meetings serve no purpose but religion," retorted Karlin, "And I'm not an evangelist."

"No one makes up her mind, changes her mind, or even speaks her mind while everyone is shouting their positions," added Soren.

"You can't reduce politics to a small group of friends," Desde objected.

"I have more faith in the durability of friendship than in an amorphous crowd held together by slogans," said Soren.

"Be quiet at the back, please. If you don't want to listen then go elsewhere."

"That's our chance," grinned Desde.

"I'm not slinking off like a guilty nelly," said Karlin.

"You can't force everyone into small groups."

"I can say what I think."

Essa was right behind Karlin. She scorned politics, that narrow hatred toward the rival gang, but as Karlin's vehicle she was righteous, untouchable. Essa steered a way through the ponderous clumps of elderly and middle old, up to the front and past the more regimented rows of furious forties. Her progress was all the more triumphal as the waves were forced to part and let the wheelchair through. All turned, like the furling leaves of the mimosa, to watch and whisper and wait.

"Megalomaniac," muttered Tessera, "Won't accept a back seat."

"Think she'd take warning from her illness."

"Brought it on herself."

"All a con if you ask me."

The oldwomen recognised Karlin despite the chair,

despite the ravines etched into her face. Her name spread through the hall with the speed of wind through dry rushes. They tried to reconcile her face with the gossip they had heard. They expected a return of the hero. They did not get one.

"I find it hard to hear in such a large crowd, let alone have my say. No one should have to fight her way to the front as I have done."

Compassionate nods.

"Knew she'd make full use of that chair," said Tessera.

"Bet she doesn't need one. I've seen her stand up when she feels like it."

"Malachi Lorluss tells me most of the other rooms are empty. I suggest we break up into small groups and report back at the end of the night."

Some oldwomen moved immediately. Others hung back, waiting to see if the idea caught on. Once it was clear the hall was emptying, Tessera's group divided up and each joined one of the discussions in the smaller rooms.

Karlin was surrounded, as of old, by Soren, Malachi, Desde and Essa. They were joined by those of the Senectity who had been around long enough to know where sense was talked.

"There is no future in blowing ourselves up," Desde announced. Her friends knew she was ticking off the slogans of the four main camps, but the sober proclamation made everyone else laugh.

"Nor do I want to kill men," she continued unabashed. "I want them to stop killing us and turning youngwomen against us."

"Youngwomen are not passive victims," Malachi insisted, "They collaborate."

"I built this city and I'm not abandoning it for a cave," Desde finished, leaving 'stay and fight' the only reputable course of action.

"The caves are occupied. They wouldn't thank us for moving in."

"Oldwomen never have had a place of our own."

"Why erase our traces? There's been rockwomen in the Scrub over three hundred years."

"One hundred."

"The question is whether we want to join them."

"The question is whether they'd let us."

"They'd make us go through the refugee camps."

"We're not refugees."

Soren felt impatient. Karlin felt Soren's impatience. Her personal small group was getting smaller and smaller.

"We stow survivors away on the underground railway," said Karlin, "What makes us think our chances here are better than theirs?"

"Most of them are escaping from Rest Homes."

Agitation spread through the room.

"Do you know what they're doing now? Filing down the residents' teeth . . . "

"Like those little nellies you see. No sooner grow their second teeth but they have them pulled. Make it easier for father."

"I know we're not here to discuss nellies, but you can't help feeling sorry for the wretches."

"Why shouldn't we talk about them?" demanded Essa, "They don't get the chance to grow old."

"They grow up, unfortunately, into youngwomen."

"We can't help everyone," said Soren, "Oldwomen are burnt, raped, murdered daily. The young who used to front for us are missing more and more rendezvous. Whole blocks are on brick to brick search. Any oldwoman sighted is sent to a Rest Home."

"That's just a propaganda exercise while the Ideo's away. To let the citizens know everything's under control. They haven't rounded us up."

"I've been in a Rest Home," said E'thane. "I wasn't allowed to have baths. The regulations said I needed an attendant, but you couldn't have an attendant unless you were bedridden. Soon I was bedridden. I lay all day in the same position, my back a sheet of bedsores. Maggots ate the pus. They say maggots are the most efficient cleansers. They said if I was nice and smiled at the fathers, I would get on better. They told me to open wide. They said they could make it easier for me to open wider and things would be even better. They said I could have a silver plate in my mouth." E'thane smiled dangerously. She put her unbandaged hand to her mouth and removed the plate. Her lips pleated inward. She rolled back the top lip to reveal her gums. Every oldwoman in the room stared helplessly at E'thane's mouth. The Tramontane had two rows of filed stumps with the property sign tattooed on the inside of her top lip.

"I escaped," she said, "But they found me. Strapped me down and cut me open, sucked my blood in glass tubes every three days."

The oldwomen had shunned E'thane on sight, clearly crazy, and probably dangerous. They did not know what to do with this spectacle of misery. So they prepared to ignore it. Their picture of the Rest Homes included humiliation and bad food, not torture and sexual slavery. They had heard of rows of oldwomen slumped in low chairs in a long room, encouraged to sing songs of civic pride along with the television. Often they sang a different song, to a different tune, a song which had been on the television the day before. The effect was eerie, but as long as the residents sang, they got their sardines.

E'thane looked at Essa for confirmation of her story. To everyone's surprise the arch-conservative nodded. Karlin was disgusted. In what tub of feathers were these oldwomen hiding their heads that this horror could be news to them? News it evidently was, or they would not oblige a Rest Home survivor to produce the physical evidence of assault. Essa should have refused the need for corroboration. By their stunned expressions it appeared that many had been considering giving themselves up. They must have worked hard to persuade themselves that Karlin and Soren exaggerated the depravity of the young. Karlin watched their faces, shocked open by pity, close over again in disbelief. It was not possible, no one could treat fragile oldpeople like that. Therefore it had not happened. Therefore the Tramontane was lying. Therefore when the worst came, it would still be feasible to give in and go quietly.

Before Karlin or Soren could capitalize on the crazy's horrifying fantasy, a new voice piped up. "Exactly. And now we're in a good position to fight back against the mistreatment of the old."

Had Karlin been ill that long? Since when had torture been called mistreatment? However, she kept quiet, waiting to learn how deep the rot had sunk.

"We're all oldwomen in the Senectity," this new voice continued, "That's what keeps us together. But we also have connections with other groups. Tessera has invited representatives of the youthful disadvantaged to meet with us in the morning. Once they realise how many we are, and how strong the Senectity, they'll . . . "

"Kill us all in one go," supplied Soren.

"Pessimism won't get us anywhere. We tried to discuss it with everyone at the general meeting, but you insisted on leaving. So don't accuse us of subterfuge."

"What time are the youths expected?" asked Soren in level tones.

"Noon. To give them time to get up and us time to prepare a statement."

"And the rest of us time to flee," put in Malachi.

"We can't go on living under stones. You've done wonders building up the Senectity, now we can make a mass movement working with all the other oppressed groups: oboes, trams, nellies, sickies, crazies . . . " She ticked them off her fingers like new varieties of ice cream.

"The only time I'm prepared to co-operate with youngwomen is when they decide to kill men," said a small but fierce voice.

"Or feed them black moss to put the Y chromosome to sleep," added her equally small but less fierce friend, "Like in the Tramontane story."

"Citizens' watch have been watching the footstools to see who comes and goes," Tessera's mouthpiece continued, "They think we're old rubbish and bag-women, but soon they'll move against us."

Karlin tried one more time. Refusing to believe the worst of your own species was such a human failing. She gazed round the room and could see the chaos and confusion which would reign at twelve noon tomorrow. For a short time. Until the last ceiling fell and the flames swept over the last charred body. Why was self-sacrifice preferable to acknowledging the existence of evil? The destruction would not be the work of youngwomen, but they would be unable to stop their youngmen.

"They are moving against us. We are plague rats eating their food, breathing their air, poisoning their city. We should have died already. Have you lived so long inside the Senectity that you have forgotten that? Because a few individuals are decent does not change the nature of the institution."

"They need us," continued Soren, "They need the old to honour their youth. They like to know the footstools exist, even if they never come here, because however difficult their lives, at least they are not old like us."

"But we do not need them," said Malachi, "We could leave the footstools and never come back. All we have is ourselves."

"That's all we ever had."

"Don't humble yourself. We have a first-class com-munication system and the city computer housing, thanks to you Malachi. We understand that you've been carrying the Senectity a long time. The rest of us have been negligent. But one can be too cynical. We need hope."

Karlin was tired. Meetings used to last all night because it was all so important. Now it was important that she last the night. In the corridor outside Karlin turned to the others.

"No surprises," said Desde.

"I'm surprised," said Karlin. "I will never become so battle-scarred that mass suicide leaves me indifferent."

"It seems we've made up our minds," said Soren.

"Why don't Soren and Essa wheel Karlin home?", suggested Malachi, "Desde and I will clear up here." Not an eyelash betrayed the irony behind the banality. In a few words all had been discussed and decided. Though many of the Senectity were wary enough to keep away from tomorrow's meeting, Tessera had not left time to change the minds of the others. It was the timing that was at issue, and timing could be tampered with. The scant words and gestures exchanged between Karlin, Soren, Malachi and Desde were enough to establish that: if Tessera had indeed been so foolhardy as to invite youngwomen to a meeting in the footstools, one at least amongst them had by now informed her youngman; once the youngmen knew, they would attempt to sabotage the meeting, and the best time to lay schemes and fuses would be the night before the meeting took place; better someone should stay up and watch, foil the saboteurs and present the evidence to the Senectity. Essa would be outraged if she knew what the four oldwomen intended, her outrage echoed by the thousand-voiced Senectity: if someone suspected a plot to blow up the footstools, she should tell everyone what she knew so they all had a chance to agree a course of action; better that Essa be whisked off, out of harm's reach.

Karlin did not object to being bundled out of the way, clearly Malachi was the best fitted to the job. It was the role of decoy Karlin disliked. Essa was a compassionate, practical oldwoman; it was wrong to puff her up with makework as though she were an oversensitive nelly who must not hear what the grown-ups are doing.

"Political imperatives are often unpopular," said Desde.

The pomp and cliché glanced off Karlin's battling conscience. They had to show the Senectity what it meant to walk into the arms of the fathers. But Karlin believed in friendship, and Essa was a friend. How could any action be good which was based on deceit between friends?

Soren's thoughts followed Karlin's and beyond. It had been so easy for the four of them to reach agreement without speaking and in front of Essa. Soren wanted that political telepathy with her lover which, analysed, amounted only to close attention and years of opinion-making.

"No," said Essa firmly, "Desde can accompany Karlin, I'm worried about E'thane."

Using aerorods, Desde guided the Quantum off the roof of the two detches, waited till Karlin and Soren were settled before joining Malachi in the footstools.

"Earned a back seat at last," laughed Soren as she and Karlin settled down to sleep.

The high pitch whirr of the dials told Malachi the concourse door had been closed and the mass meeting was over. The beginning of the long wait. As the hours passed, and no one came, a miracle danced in her mind. The youngwomen had not told the fathers of the noonday rendezvous. They had realised they had more to gain than fear from the Senectity; that it was in their interests not to betray the oldwomen. The miracle was followed by doom. Malachi waited in vain; the fathers had mined the footstools from the outside, infiltrating through vents and ducts and would not come near the place. The only hope of warning her peers of the danger was in recording the actions of the fathers. Malachi hoped the fathers would not come, she wanted to believe in coalition.

"The Senectity turned against Karlin as soon as she got ill," whispered Desde, attempting natural conversation to ease the burden of waiting.

"No," said Malachi, "It was when she sent her young lover away. They had always liked her for that one obvious weakness; sleeping with a youngwoman was a breach of integrity they approved."

"But Karlin always said individual youngwomen could be trusted."

"You know the Senectity. A lot of them like their politics simple. Old: good; young: bad. Then they can find flaws."

"Love you more for the flaw than the rest?"

"I don't know. A lot of oldwomen got scared they'd stuck their necks out too far. With Karlin ill they could pull in without losing face."

The screen in the main gallery lit up. The fathers had arrived: ten good men and true, and a small arsenal for courage. Four levels below, Malachi could smell their fear and their sweat. They looked like all the fathers who run for buses, stock up on sugarfix and urinate in toilets. Pleasant youngmen with the gentlest of eyes. They stuck close together, a twenty-legged, ten-headed, hip-brained beast. With great surprise Malachi watched them go right past the corridor leading to the concourse, which was the quickest way into the footstools, and tramp on to the lift shaft. They walked through the false back wall of the lift cage and prepared to slide down the conveyor belt. Tessera had shown more forethought than they'd credited her with. She must have told the youngwomen this was the only entrance, wanting to be warned well in advance, by the unmistakeable noise, when the youth representatives arrived. It seemed not even the fathers had thought to examine the plan of the building.

The long drop in the eerie silence seemed to unnerve the invaders.

"Only ten of them," whispered Desde, "By the look of what they're carrying they didn't have access to the high-tec toys. I'd say it's a small branch of citizens' watch trying out for glory."

"Long live small fry," said Malachi.

"Run the wire down the main corridor and through the leads at the end: that'll increase the spread. Keep the nitro two point one, no stronger. We want to bomb the lower levels and seal them, but leave the tower intact. No laurels for destroying the après-ski into the bargain. The bodies have to be recognisable so we can do a count. Rewards go on numbers, remember."

"Don't get ideas, Desde," said Malachi, "If we touch those fathers someone will come to find out why."

"Set the timers for one o'clock; make sure everyone's nicely inside and sitting comfortably."

"Whoever they are. Oldwomen couldn't have built all this. I'd say it's the Tramontane fathers avenging the firebombs."

"Could be the little sisters have lied to us, so hurry up and let's get out of here."

"That's it?" Desde asked Malachi incredulously.

"Laid their fuses, planted their explosives, wired their gas sprays with clockwork order, then left," breathed Malachi. "Took them exactly ten minutes."

"How long's it going to take us to dismantle?"

"We're going to leave everything just as it is," said Malachi.

Desde stared at her.

"Except the timers. The ceilings are going to fall in, the doors will be blasted out, glass splinters will spray everywhere, and the whole of the footstools will be filled with monoxide. Just as the fathers planned. Only instead of all this destruction at one o'clock in the afternoon, it's going to happen half an hour from now."

"Tessera will say it was us."

"And everyone else will have the nasty suspicion it wasn't."

Twenty Fifth Sighting: THE LAST DEATH
OF PATIENT Y

The distance, the resourcefulness, the patience ground down into her bones. Instead of a companion almost autistic in her independence, Zay would have preferred a weak and whining equal. Ithaca's height and strength drew lovers like a lodestone, the discovery of fierce intelligence secured their interest but it was her solitude which kept them buzzing back long after the relationship was through. This itemised explanation of her charms Ithaca offered Zay with sadness bordering arrogance. She needed no one. Like a hundred others before her, Zay was sure she was the one Ithaca could not live without. From harsh concrete blossoms romance full-blown.

Released from the prison of testing rock and watching loose shale fly down the mountainside now that they had reached the flats, Zay's mind was free to wander the skyline. It remained fixed on Ithaca. Independence was a scar on the elasticity of her body; in pronouncing her free of need, it reinforced her inflexibility.

As they neared the city, though Zay longed for the speed of skates and streets, the old urge, half-doused with carefully built contempt, raised its peremptory head; she wanted to belong, she wanted to be necessary.

The citizens, awakening to the news that a gang of Tramontanes had blown up the base of the Après-Ski Tower, failed to notice when the Ideo Logician passed silently through the south gate and inside the walls of the city. The bells chimed mid-day on deserted streets, the glass towers sparkled like fresh rinsed decanters, even the litter bins glistened emptily, like a new town, factory-fresh, awaiting its first inhabitants. Only the water, playing in the fountains, surging up the lift shafts, flowing in gutters so clean you could see right to the bottom of the deep blue gutter-bed, was alive and moving. Until Ithaca, raising the receiver of a public telephone to let Karlin know of her arrival, caught a citizens warning loop.

> "Return home and stay indoors. Plug in your
> autobar for all vital services. A civic crisis has
> been declared. Credits will be covered by the
> municipality."

Zay picked up the last newspaper on a vendor's barrow: "Revolt"

Together they ran down the middle of the road, the white line marked out like a path before them. Way above their heads came the eerie sound of a whistle. It followed them along each turning of the road, accompanied, sometimes, by the clatter of feet along the galleries which connect the glass towers. As Ithaca and Zay burst into Karlin's building, the whistle stopped short and silence poured like lead. They stayed only long enough to establish that Karlin had gone. A plastic bag full of bread hung from the kitchen window, still fresh. Ithaca picked it up as an emblem of hope. Someone had expected to be hungry. Someone had expected to live.

As the revolving door swung them back out into the street, the whistle started again. Sometimes they glimpsed a figure standing at the end of a gallery, fore-fingers to his lips. All roads led to the Après-Ski Tower. To a stage set for race riot. The base of the tower had been blackened by fire, holes gaped in the fabric of the building, windows had been blown out into the city square, dust from the rubble hovered in a red haze and white ash fluttered in the air. Water from firewatch hoses ran in an endless stream down the marble staircase, a clean black line amid the dust and ashes. With a gurgle it flowed over the bottom step and formed a gulley through the debris.

Ithaca and Zay stood still, hands on bent knees, panting like athletes. Out of the mouth of the Tower came two oldwomen, one leaning heavily against the other. They shuffled forward to the top step and over to the hose pipe. The explosion had ripped an enormous lump of concrete out of the side of the building and hurled it onto the marble. One oldwoman loosed her grip on the other and let her companion down gently onto the lump of concrete. The companion jerked uncontrollably and the oldwoman was obliged to hook both her friend's elbows round the reinforced steel prongs to keep her upright. Once the companion was seated, the oldwoman tore a strip of rag from the bandage on her own wrist, wet it and wiped both their faces. Holding the hose between her knees, she cupped one hand, filled her palm with water and made her companion drink.

Like climbers who had stopped briefly to rest on a hot day, the two oldwomen soon got to their feet and continued down the steps. Their progress was difficult. The constant jerking of the one placed an added burden on the other. Only when the oldwoman seemed to lose her grip on her companion did Ithaca leap to her feet, Zay only a shadow behind. As the four women reached the bottom step, a wave of fury broke over the streets.

The doors of the city opened, citizens poured out carrying knives, guns, petrol bombs, axes, any defensive weapon they could lay hands on. Forlorn groups of Tramontanes, whom hunger and thirst had forced back into the city, stood in the outer circle waiting for papers to be stamped and passes allocated. A tableau of misery. Like a reflection in a pond after the first pebble has been thrown, the frame was broken, the composition shattered. A skip transporter hurtled toward the outsiders and they fled, straight into the arms of the mob. They were picked up and thrown bodily over the side of the transporter and fell to the stinking bottom of the city skip. Further on citizens held Zay and the two oldwomen like trophies above the heads of the crowd. As the transporter neared the Après-Ski Tower the trophies were tossed in among the other derelicts.

Few citizens spared a second glance at Ithaca, enormous though she was, wondering only what weapon she carried. It was all she could do to keep pace with the transporter. As it accelerated once more, and was about to lurch away, Ithaca leapt over the side. Tramontane faces, dirty and desperate, turned toward the citizen.

"They threw you in too?"

"No," said Ithaca, "I jumped."

A slight shifting of positions, of weight from one leg to another, an assiduous attention to the injured, produced a marked distance, even in the crowded, filthy skip, between those who had been thrown and she who had jumped.

"Where's this thing headed?" asked Ithaca.

Shoulders shrugged.

"Central booster," murmured Zay softly.

"Where they process the slurry," said the oldwoman with the bandaged wrist, "The ooze that's left after the rubbish is recycled." She smiled, revealing rotten stubs of teeth which slithered on the word 'slurry' with dangerous delight. Zay looked at her crazy, laughing face; looked at the faces of the people whom fate, or lynching citizens, had thrown with her into the skip. There was an incongruous levity in their eyes. This was not a cattle truck to the abattoir, but a guerilla train to the heart of enemy headquarters. Zay threw back her head and whooped, clicked her tongue against the back of her tooth ridge and trilled in descending scale. There was at first no sign or movement from the crowd. Then a flicker, a rustle, one high, muffled ululation, and, finally, four distinct raps on the side of the skip.

"Let's go," she said to Ithaca, "Quick, before they change their minds."

Ithaca looked baffled.

"The women say we can go, as long as we take the two old ones with us. If we hang back the men will overrule them."

"Jacknife bend at the end of the access slipway off the northbound conduit, it'll slow us almost to standstill," said the oldwoman with the bandaged wrist, "We should step off then."

Ithaca didn't move.

"Pull those bolts out from the end panel," the oldwoman instructed, "Then heave open your side. You'll have to crack the welds. Get your shoulder in there; muscles like yours, you can do it."

Ithaca realised she was being flirted with and responded with mock bravado, pretending strain and force to make it look difficult. The oldwoman replied in role.

"You may be able to leap over, but me and my friend are far too little." Then, sure that the enormous one would obey, "Push the panel out so we can slide to the ground."

War between the fathers meant a healthy loss of brutal youngmen, as long as the battleground was far away. But killing each other put fresh blood on their tongue, unleashed unparalleled cruelty on the women within reach. Someone must get rid of fathers or the oldwomen would never get to the refugee camps, the youngwomen would never grow up, not even the rockwomen would be safe in their caves. E'thane, with the wisdom of the crazy, the wisdom of ages, the wisdom of suffering, the wisdom of the Tramontane, all the arcane wisdoms in which she or anyone believed, E'thane knew that she was the one. She looked closely at the three women chosen to share the moment.

"Do you know Karlin Miray?" Ithaca asked the old Tramontane once they were safely off the skip. "She's an oldwoman . . . "

E'thane interrupted her, "And as I'm old myself, I'll know all the others?"

"She's very ill . . . and very small . . . ," Ithaca continued, "And very beautiful."

"What's it to you?"

"I'm her lover," said Ithaca, half boast, half confession. Unthinkable to say 'she's my lover' as she had of Zay. She could describe herself in relation to Karlin, but not the other way round.

"I mean, what's it worth?"

"Tchai," Zay interrupted Ithaca's next prevarication. "Enough fresh tchai to toast the four of us every day for a month."

"I'd have to taste it," said E'thane.

Zay untied the sack on Ithaca's back and pulled out a lump of the black moss spores they had taken from the rockwomen's silo. E'thane examined it.

"Just what I've been looking for," she said.

On the centre island between north and southbound conduits, on grass a hundred years untrampled, E'thane prepared the toast in the ancient way.

"Here's bread to cut with it," offered Ithaca, pulling the plastic bag from the sack.

"Good," said E'thane, "Youngfriend been giving you lessons in Tramontane ritual?"

"No," said Ithaca, "My mother."

E'thane shrugged and divided the toast into three. "So," she said, "Who am I toasting?"

"Zay Liebling and Ithaca Benaccar," said Zay, bowing formally.

"Patient Y," E'thane gestured toward her companion, "and E'thane Tramontane."

Ithaca stared at the oldwoman in horror, and then at Zay.

"No," said Zay, laughing at the idea, then, more seriously watching Ithaca's face, "Didn't you know? I always thought you were being discreet. 'E'thane' is

176

the word for oldwoman in Tramontane. In the city they use it to protect individual identity."

"Your mother didn't teach you very much," observed E'thane.

On the surface, relief and disappointment vied with each other for command of Ithaca. Nearer in she felt the foundations of the known world shift in their rockbed. If even her mother's name had been a lie, what was true and how could she recognise it? She and Athos were different from the other zappers because they had a mother, despised, barbaric custom, but a link with what had gone before them. And now it seemed the name she called upon silently to help and guide her was the name for all oldwomen.

"Outside the city old people are revered; did you not know that either?"

No, Ithaca knew nothing any more.

"You can't stay there and refuse to play because you've been lied to," said Zay. "We're sitting in a war zone and you're on the other side."

"Where's Karlin?" Ithaca demanded roughly of E'thane, roused to act on someone else's behalf. "You promised you'd tell us what you know."

"She's where I'd be if I had any sense," E'thane replied, "Fleeing to the refugee camps."

"I don't believe you," said Ithaca, "But I'll follow you till I find her."

E'thane shrugged again and made the toast in silence. Fortified by the life-giving smoke, which filled her lungs and nose, she got to her feet and, supporting Patient Y with her good arm, crossed the northbound conduit to the fence which protected the central booster.

The perimeter fence was garlanded with the usual testaments to youth. Nappies, bootees, rattles and blue fluffy blankets swung on the wire, ruffled by the breeze. Every twelfth a roster of youngwomen came with fresh supplies, tributes to the clean quiet power of the booster which daily released raw energy from coal, gas and atomic fission, and harvested it as electricity.

Behind the fence was gathered the Tramontane army. Sheer righteousness had plunged the transporters through the base defences. Nature itself, revolting against the harness which perverted and bound it to the vicious uses of the city, had embraced the liberators with open arms. They lolled on the lawn of the oppressors. No trace of citizen struggle, no trace of citizens at all: a bloodless revolution.

"Those who control the power, control the city," observed E'thane.

"And they're comfy cosy, safe inside the booster," said Ithaca, "waiting for the best moment to lay waste the Tramontanes," an adult sugaring the lesson the naive nelly should have learned years ago.

"How do we get in?" asked E'thane.

"You can't," emphatic adult.

"You can," wheedling nelly.

"Yes," adult closing the matter.

"We need a nuclear explosion," said E'thane bluntly.

Ithaca laughed. "You'd die before you reached the fission chamber. There isn't a button you press from an armchair to make the whole world go boom."

"There's a nuclear warning alarm."

"Not the same thing at all."

"Who's to know that, in the middle of a civil war?"

"You want everyone to panic?"

"Women don't panic. We're too used to crises. It's the fathers will react."

"They're unlikely to commit mass suicide. Probably reach for a gas mask and a prophylactic."

E'thane nodded.

"What's the point?" snapped Zay, "What're you going to do? Slip something nasty in their condoms?"

E'thane chuckled. "Not me. Patient Y."

Patient Y shook uncontrollably.

"She wouldn't make it past the first sonar," said Ithaca, irritable adult tiring of nelly's game. "The sonars are tuned to the heart. All official heartbeats are keyed in; when someone passes, they search their memories for a match. If they don't find one they shoot."

"Patient Y doesn't have a heart," said E'thane.

Ithaca looked at Zay, exasperated. Best go back to the city and find Karlin on their own.

E'thane smiled winningly. "Tell me where the alarm bells are, and I'll tell you where Karlin is right now."

"You first."

"Karlin Miray is sitting in a wheelchair in a silver Quantum Libet on her way to Interim Two with Soren Kesh, Essa Foujad, Malachi Lorluss and Desde Izquierda."

E'thane leaned against the cement slab they were hiding behind, pursed her lips and waited. Ithaca bent over the side of the slab, put her hand to a small steel plate concealed beneath a brick. She raised the cover of a storm drain, revealing an underground tunnel.

"You'll never make it," she repeated, "but the nearest alarm is on the other side of the base. Follow this tunnel, however it twists and turns back on itself; where it finally splits in a T junction there's a row of red buttons. I'd press them all for a really impressive result."

"Then what?" asked Zay, wanting a satisfying conclusion.

"The sirens will fill the air with black moss spores," said E'thane matter-of-factly, beginning to roll another toast with her good hand.

"She'll hardly have enough tchai left for a day's worth of toasts," whispered Zay, "The way she's getting through it, she's the most likely to succumb."

"It's to put the Y chromosome to sleep," E'thane finished.

"As you'd put a crying baby to sleep?" Ithaca asked jocularly.

"Or a rabid dog?" Zay added.

"Well," said E'thane, prodding the smouldering tchai with a sharp blade, "What would you say? Are fathers more like crying babies or rabid dogs?"

E'thane grinned, drawing her upper lip back from her teeth so that the rotten stumps and brand were visible. Ithaca was bent toward her, a tower leaning over an anthill. At E'thane's elbow the body of Patient Y shook and from time to time, for no apparent reason, her knees jerked or her arms shot out. This was a person said to have no heart, a mechanical instrument built for a purpose. Its eyes were as dead as fish, but its face was that of a woman, its limbs were spotted with age and its back was bent to suggest the decay of senescence. Why make a robot like a sick oldwoman? Were not the sick and unsightly often said to be dead already, dead to all intents and purposes, to excuse treating their bodies as corpses? E'thane caught Zay's gaze, fixed on Patient Y.

"Don't like the idea of female sacrifice?" she asked sarcastically, "Does this make the destruction of the fathers more palatable?" and she grabbed a lump of Patient Y's hair, tore it away from Y's head, and peeled off a layer of skin down her forehead, over the bridge of her nose, stopping at her upper lip. The skin and hair hung in a thin coil over Patient Y's chin exposing a block of hard, welded steel.

As Zay and Ithaca stared at the shiny metal of Y's head, E'thane, quick as a flash, quick as an oldwoman with a job to do, shoved a tchai-laden piece of rag over their noses. In less than two they fell to the ground, an intoxicated heap like all the joyjoys in all the city doorways. E'thane released Ithaca from the sack she had been carying and hooked it round Patient Y's steel shoulder. In less than a month all the men in the city, all the men in the hinterland, citizen or Tramontane, would be asleep.

Twenty Sixth Sighting: A GIFT OF TCHAI

The Quantum was half-way through the northern portal when they heard the first explosion. Then came a series of whipcracks. Desde drove on, keeping clear of flyovers and aerial conduits, just in case. As the car wound its way round the last of the loop oneways, there was a deafening crash. A white cloud swallowed the city centre. Half an hour later fine ash swirled in the air, covering the windscreen in a soft blanket.

Since their departure the oldwomen had been sealed tight in separate silences, trying to absorb the enormity of what they were doing. Karlin loved the city of glass and water, the beauty of skateboards and traffic; she would not easily have left it for the salad splendour of the countryside. It seemed almost fitting that the day she left, the city should cease to be. If it burst into spontaneous flame and burnt itself out, her memories need never be updated. Essa, seated beside the wheelchair, was furious that they'd acted behind her back, turned up at her flat door and invited her to come with them. As if she'd had any choice. The column of smoke and dust which hovered over the city was a hideous 'I told you so'. It was easier than the relief she might have felt that she had not been trapped in the footstools; easier than the horror which

181

would otherwise swallow her like the dust cloud. Soren wanted time to be alone with Essa, to think and talk and act as one person again, instead of an army. Whatever life would be like in the refugee camps, it was sure to require collectivity of soul. Soren wanted to snuggle down in a little cottage in the hinterland with wisteria over the door and be a good person, quietly.

"Whole Après-Ski Tower must have gone up," said Malachi. It might be self-evident, but it papered the silence.

"Where's the sense in that?" asked Desde, straining to see through the thick grey slush. She jetted water onto the windscreen in an attempt to clear it, succeeded only in mixing the ash with the red dust, forming an increasingly opaque mudpack. As the wipers struggled to force a passage they compacted the mud and scratched the glass. There was very little traffic about, and she had picked a careful route through the backstreets, but still, it would be nice to be able to see where she was going. Marvellous how no one else noticed her heroism.

"Miscalculation," said Malachi, wondering whether she too had been at fault. "They used too much nitro."

"You can't kill the oldwomen in the basement without bringing the rest of the Tower down," said Soren.

They were out in the hinterland now, threading a slow progress along the byways. The pace and route would make them look like pleasure trippers. But there was no-one to look. Karlin gazed anxiously out of the window, wishing Soren could see what she saw. She could describe it to her old friend, but not without panic waves from Essa. Every Tramontane township they passed was empty. No women with babies on their backs pounded meal. No nellies sang and beat clothes on the river rocks. The fields were empty though the crop was ripe. Fleeing themselves, the oldwomen should know the condition of the land they passed through. Had the civic unrest unleashed revolution?

"The fathers who mined the footstools," said Essa slowly, "Who were they, Malachi?"

"Local Citizens' Watch," said Malachi, "Small fry."

"Not Tramontanes?" pursued Essa, surveying the same dead landscape which bothered Karlin.

"It's quiet alright," said Soren.

Karlin had a sudden rush of love for both her old friend and, unexpectedly, the uncharming Essa. They too had noticed the deserted hinterland, they too were wondering about the second, thunderous explosion. Life after the luxury car came to a stop would be that much easier if they could continue to guess in synchrony.

"Better for us if all the fathers are engaged in the city," said Malachi.

"The first wave of a new exodus," said Desde, "Aren't we important." She had been driving for hours and her vision was limited to a small wedge of windscreen the wipers were managing to scrape clear. No doubt the intellectuals in the back would be able to offer a suitable metaphor. The Quantum was heavy and crowded with five oldwomen, a wheelchair and the two hundred boxes of computer scree Malachi had insisted they stow in the hatch.

"In fifty years no one will say there never were oldwomen in the city," Malachi had put her foot down. "I've got a full colour tape of the fathers laying the fuses, in case any of our lot are still in doubt."

Karlin was still in doubt as to who 'our lot' were. The lumps of wretched humanity plucked by the Senectity from the operating trolleys which rattled through the footstools had only age or sickness in common with her. She missed Ithaca's strength, her obstinacy, her brave, thrashing efforts at integrity. Ithaca was neither old nor ill, but Karlin loved her, would trust her with more than she'd let many an oldwoman glimpse. It made her happy that Ithaca was crazy about her, but the secret of Karlin's generation gap romance was that Ithaca understood what to be crazy about. There was always some new hopeful hovering in the wings, in love with Karlin's brains, or her political acumen. Ithaca loved her for her body and because she was good. The Senectity was not an organisation against the young, but for the old. How had that distinction become blurred? The youngwoman on roller skates in the toilets, months ago, or maybe yesterday; she had been scared, disgusted by Karlin's old body. But she too had wanted to be good, had risked city censure to do what was right. And she danced like a dream. Karlin had not forgotten how the youngwoman waltzed her down the high kerb to the car. How many points did one give for effort? There were surely fathers in the city residences who had never touched their nellies or their zappers; who had behaved decently to the Tramontane nursemaids, and honourably to colleagues. The Senectity's careful analyses were not about to be blown away by the introduction of the first well-behaved youngman. Nevertheless, what relief to wake one morning and discover some mad woman had gone out with a machine gun and shot them all, so they would not prey upon your flesh, or your conscience, again.

The road skirted the northbound conduit, a service track which veered off toward the mountains in the shadow of the hanging gazibus. A suitably nothing place to stop and rest. Desde moved the levers which would lower Karlin's chair to ground level. In a moment the crowded quantum emptied. In a hollow by the perimeter fence of the central booster sat an oldwoman with a bandaged arm. Essa was almost unsurprised. All oldwomen were fleeing the city; it stretched coincidence only slightly that the Quantum's first hitch hiker should be one whom it appeared Essa's life work to rescue. That she should be accompanied by Karlin's young lover, and the lover's even younger ex-lover, would have been an event worth commenting on, had not the siren sounded for a nuclear alert.

184

Ithaca lay in the hatch with Karlin. The wheelchair was strapped to the roof of the Quantum, Zay and E'thane were squeezed in next to Essa, two hundred boxes of computer scree lay buried under the grass between the north and southbound conduits, destined to remain untrodden for another fifty years. Overhead the sirens released a million black moss spores into the air. E'thane's gift of tchai.

Ithaca turned toward her lover. She was going to tell her everything; about the wind tunnel and the rockwomen, Scimitel and the black moss; she wanted Karlin to know everything. She was going to say, "I'm glad you're alive", "I'm glad you're better." But Karlin was gazing at her with such fond pleasure that Ithaca kept quiet.

Ithaca looked exactly as though she had been for a brisk four day hike over the mountains. As she began to have strength for more than the bare essentials of living, Karlin had regaled herself with a hundred and one scenes of reunion with Ithaca. Her imagination had not once come up with the hatch of a speeding Quantum, though the cramped quarters and low roof acted as a remarkable leveller. Ithaca's legs were obliged to fold back on themselves like stacked deckchairs; her height and hugeness were less obvious lying down. Karlin, weary of confinement, nevertheless found the narrow hatch a comfort to her narrowed scope.

Ithaca stroked a finger down Karlin's cheek, feeling both brave and impudent. The skin stretched tight over bone, until her finger reached Karlin's neck where she found soft flaps with no flesh to fill them.

"I'm afraid I'll hurt you," she said.

"So am I," said Karlin, "Both ways."

To remove Karlin's apparel, Ithaca had to open the sunroof, arch her back, raise Karlin with one arm, and slip the garment over her shoulders with the other. She had planned to spread herself over her lover's body gradually, with enough time and attention to recognise her underneath the obvious changes. Now here was Karlin suddenly in her arms, weighing less than Scimitel, with less bulk than the sack of moss she had carried over the mountains. Ithaca was shocked. Karlin seemed not to be a person, there was so little of her left. She hoped Karlin had not felt the pity, horror and pain which coursed through her then, realising what irony it was that she should wish Karlin to miss part of what she was doing. Only their full attention would bring them close again. There were some thoughts, however, which one ought to hide.

Karlin had caught the lapse in attentions paid to her. As Ithaca ran her hand along the inside of Karlin's calf, secretly aghast at how quickly the muscle had turned to soft putty, Karlin snapped.

"I don't want to be weighed, measured and pitied, Ithaca. I want to be loved."

"Do you?" said Ithaca quietly, "And do you love me?"

The bitterness of Karlin's illness burned an acid line between them. Ithaca hung like a heavy shadow over the bed. She would hear Karlin's little bell and jerk awake, stumble to her feet and come to find out what her lover needed. Often she discovered the bell had not been rung, Karlin needed nothing but the sleep which had been interrupted by Ithaca's solicitous enquiries. Ithaca still heard the bell in her dreams; lying out in mountain caves with Zay, the bell would ring and she would struggle, half asleep, to get to Karlin. Soren had told her she must go home and rest, she was no use to anyone anxious, tired and fretful, but Ithaca would reply that she would worry about Karlin wherever she stayed and only at her lover's bedside could she know what her condition was. Then Soren told her she must leave room for others to sleep at Karlin's overnight, the flat was small and Karlin needed more than Ithaca could provide. The day she was to justify the low priority she had given to raising male and lowering female birth rates, was the day Karlin had started vomiting again and it seemed she would not last the night. Ithaca had set out for the Benaccar Residence where the lines were open and waiting. Somewhere in the background of her mind, where there was room for thoughts unattached to Karlin, Ithaca knew it was vital to the female population of the city that more nellies be born than zappers. She had sat down at her terminal, accessed justification mode, and punched in HIGH-MALE SEX-QUOTAS: LOW PRIORITY quickly and correctly. If she could do it all without thinking, she might get through. The fathers' terminal responded immediately, repeating her formula in the interrogative and adding, as expected, JUSTIFICATION AWAITED. Why? Ithaca had wondered. Why should they not raise the birth ratio in favour of youngmen? What was it to her? She'd already been born. Her cynicism surprised her, the best quality for an Ideo, yet she had thought loving Karlin had taken it out of her. The only answer she came up with to the formula on her screen was that otherwise Karlin would die. She could not punch that in; it wasn't true. Age and illness were killing Karlin, not the fathers. Once she had let Karlin into her study, Ithaca was lost, as obsessed with her lover as all the silly zappers she had scorned in the compound. Her independence was in shreds, she was incompetent for this simple task and without her exalted position as Logician she was a laughable oddity who would soon be stoned to death. When Soren had asked her to go to the Scrub, Ithaca had taken the hero's option and the martyr's farewell. She was losing her job, her city and perhaps her life for an oldwoman who did not love her.

Karlin, so much older than Ithaca, was doomed to feel acutely both her lover's plight and her own. She was responsible for the change in Ithaca because she had caused it to happen. She had filled her lover with purpose and committment, spoiling her for her job whose main qualification was haughty cynicism. It was because of Karlin that the Quantum was now carrying two youngwomen to live among the old.

What good would it do them to be always with those who had thought their thoughts before them? Karlin saw Ithaca's shadow again, looming, begging silently, "Why don't you love me? You ought to love me. Please, before you die, just say you do. It doesn't matter if it isn't true". Karlin had been incensed. Did Ithaca think death was a romantic interlude? a pretext on which everything must be granted? When Karlin had indeed felt herself weakening to the point where there seemed no life left, everyone had crowded in, ordering her to stay alive for their sake. When she began to revive, in small, secret stages, then they had accused her of wanting to die, of killing herself with neglect. They meant 'neglect of them'. They put it to her that Ithaca's presence was dangerous; they meant 'dangerous to them'. Karlin had wanted to spare Ithaca the pain of watching her lover deteriorate, and herself the pain of having her lover watch. It was a mistake she regretted as soon as Ithaca had gone. This saving for best was not the relationship she wanted. They would mean so much more to each other now had they both lived through her illness; no need of this embattled reunion.

"I'm concerned about you," Karlin said at last.

"It's not the same," said Ithaca but she reached out toward Karlin anyway, and, with as much gentleness as there was room for, pulled her lover on top of her. Karlin's cheek lay against hers; Ithaca was overwhelmed with tenderness. It was surely impossible for such strong feelings to remain unreturned for long.

RADICAL FEMINIST & LESBIAN PUBLISHERS

poetry

theory

science fiction

debate

novels

love stories

and

GOSSIP: a journal of lesbian feminist ethics

for free catalogue write to:

ONLYWOMEN PRESS
38 Mount Pleasant
London WC1X 0AP